THE WHITE VAN

THE
WHITE VAN

Patrick Hoffman

Atlantic Monthly Press
New York

This book is a work of fiction. Names, characters, places, and incidents are products of the author's imagination. Any resemblance to actual events, locales, entities, or persons living or dead are entirely coincidental.

Published simultaneously in Canada
Printed in the United States of America

FIRST EDITION

ISBN: 978-0-8021-2304-6
eISBN: 978-0-8021-9229-5

Atlantic Monthly Press
an imprint of Grove/Atlantic, Inc.
154 West 14th Street
New York, NY 10011

Distributed by Publishers Group West

www.groveatlantic.com

14 15 16   10 9 8 7 6 5 4 3 2 1

For Nana and Patricia Coyne

PART I

1

The man who had been following her stepped into the bar. Emily remembered that. At the time she didn't know he had been following her, but she remembered the way he had stepped into the bar. She remembered the door opening. She remembered him backing into the bar and closing the door. She remembered him turning to face the bar. He was big and white and dressed like someone who had a job in an office. He hesitated at the doorway and then continued in.

Emily was sitting in the back. An old Chinese man sat toward the front. There was only the bar and fifteen stools, nothing fancy. The bartender, a woman with thick makeup, seemed happy to see the new man. She greeted him with a smile. It was a Tuesday night. There were only four people in the Kum Bak Klub.

"I'll have a whiskey," said the man, having already looked toward Emily's drink and seen something brown. There was just enough light to make out the color of it. The man had an accent of some kind. An accent and a silver watch. That was a lot. She looked him over. He seemed handsome. He was a big guy with a watch in the Tenderloin. Maybe he was here for a convention or something. He sat on his stool and sipped his drink. She sized him up.

Emily was thirty-one years old. Her hair was pulled back tight in a ponytail; she had on tight blue jeans, men's basketball shoes, and a red 49ers jacket with gold trim and snap buttons. She was pretty, but in a beat-up way. She would have been prettier in a different life. She had on black eyeliner. Her teeth were not straight, or white. Her nails were bitten down. She had a star-shaped scar on her forehead.

She sat there and watched the man's reflection in the mirror until she got distracted by the baseball game on the television. The Giants were playing; the playoffs were coming, and it was cold outside; San Francisco weather. The bartender and the old man near the door watched the game, too. Later she tried to remember how they had started talking. He was doing something. He had been writing in a notebook.

"You writing a memo?" she'd asked.

The man said, "I know it's rude to work in a bar." He put the pen back into his jacket pocket.

Emily barely understood what he had said. She heard the words but only vaguely. "It's all right," she said. She waved her hand toward him the way people talking in bars do. "You could keep doing it."

"Excuse me?" he said.

"Where you from? France?"

"I am from St. Petersburg, Russia. You know it?"

"Of course I know it," Emily said, staring at the TV. She fixed her posture a little more straight.

"Would you like another drink?" he asked.

THE WHITE VAN

"Yeah. I'll buy it, though."

"Please, I insist."

"All right, but I can only have one more," she said.

He moved a seat closer to her, leaving an empty seat between them. The drink came and after a minute he got her another. They talked haltingly at first and then more fluidly. He told her he did real estate. He said he was staying at a hotel south of the city, near the airport. She lied and told him she was a social worker. She said she helped people with drug problems. It was cold here, he said. She agreed, it was cold.

They drank more. He switched to Hennessy, saying he had never tried it. She asked him questions and answered his with a laugh. The bartender turned on the jukebox and they listened to Chinese pop music. People came and left the bar. He kept buying drinks. The bartender looked on happily.

After a while Emily announced that he was her *ace boon coon*. He said that she was his *milaya moya*. The bartender tried to teach them one of the songs. He tried to teach them a Russian song. They were drunk and he leaned on her and she leaned on him.

"You don't help people with drugs," he said. "Come on?"

"I ain't lying," she said.

She could smell cabbage on his breath. She could see the pores on his nose. They watched a loud guy come into the bar and leave.

"Have you tried drugs?" he asked.

She nodded.

"Have you tried cocaine?" he asked.

"You a cop?" she said.

"I'm Russian," he said. He tried to laugh it off.

5

"You a KGB?"

"No, I'm curious," he said. They smiled, nodded, and shifted. Their legs touched.

"I've tried it," she said, leaning her head closer to his. "Why, let me guess, you wanna try it?"

"Perhaps, I don't know—yes," he said. He measured every reaction she gave. He had only one intention and that was to get her back to his hotel. That was the starting point, get her to the hotel.

Emily made her own calculations. He didn't move like a cop. Emily didn't trust anyone, but he didn't seem dangerous. He had money, he paid for every drink; he had a nice watch, clean shoes, clean hair, clean face, nice-looking wallet. He wasn't grabby, he wasn't drunk. Doing drugs with him seemed like a good idea.

"Perhaps? Yes?" she asked, looking at him with her eyebrows arched up.

"In point of fact," said the Russian, "my friend gave me this." He reached into his front pocket and palmed a plastic bag filled with crack rocks.

"Hell no," she said. "Put that away, stupid!"

They left the bar, Emily feeling certain she had hustled him, the Russian feeling certain of the opposite.

The hotel was a Ramada on the east side of South San Francisco, on Airport Boulevard. It was surrounded by other hotels and dark, empty office buildings. The taxi driver took them back and forth down twisting roads until he found it. Emily, drunk, loud, and nervous, kept making the driver turn the music up. She rapped along with the radio: *I wear my stunna glasses at night.*

The Russian already had a room. He walked directly into a center courtyard and out through the far corner. She followed him up a flight of stairs: room 214. *Lucky 214*, she thought, touching her knuckles to the wooden door as she entered.

The room was empty and clean. Emily was nervous. The Russian had become quiet and businesslike.

"Nice place," she said.

"Very nice."

"So what's up, stupid?"

"Excuse me," said the Russian. He fished into his pocket and pulled out the plastic baggie: a quarter ounce of crack. He weighed it in his hand. "Relax," he said.

"All right," Emily said, taking off her jacket and throwing it onto a chair. "But I ain't a prostitute."

"Please, no. I didn't—I am not interested in that." He sounded English now. "I'm just here to have a good time, I assure you. Party. You know, do-duh-do-doo," he said, making a dancing gesture with his head, hands, and shoulders.

"As long as we're on the same page."

"The exact same page. Don't worry, I—I have beers in the refrigerator. Relax, please, first—it's fine, I tell you I am not even sleeping in this room." He waved at her like he was shutting her up and went on. "I have it, but for . . . funny reasons—you know, work—I have another room, too." He went to the refrigerator and handed her a bottle of beer.

"They got a radio in here?"

The Russian looked around the room. "I don't know," he said, and then, "Just TV." He turned on the television and opened a beer for himself. "Just TV and fun."

Emily sipped her beer. She was drunk already, but the quietness of the room was sobering her up. "You got a pipe?" she asked.

"Of course," he said. He reached into his jacket pocket, pulled out a brand-new glass pipe, and handed the bag to her. Emily examined the rocks; they looked fine. They were big and yellowish-brownish-white like parmesan cheese. She pinched off half of a rock with her thumbnail, put it into the pipe, and sat down on a tall chair that looked like a throne.

"So, you don't mind if I?" she asked.

He handed her a green lighter. She took two hits, blew out smoke, leaned forward, her mind opening up, and handed the pipe to the Russian. He was still standing. He took the pipe awkwardly, flinching when he grabbed the wrong end. He took the lighter from her, then walked over to a chair near the desk and sat down. He seemed nervous. Emily's own nerves had been calmed by the drug. The room had a nice warm light, and the Russian, who a few seconds earlier had looked a little scary with his big shoulders, his creviced face and big hands, now seemed friendly, maybe even pitiful. He lit the pipe, barely sucked in, and blew out a small cloud of smoke.

"Thank you," he said, standing up and handing the pipe to her.

"That's right," she said. She looked at him and nodded like a teacher pleased with a student.

She smoked the pipe and passed it back and he did the same. They went back and forth like this for a while, drinking beers in between and talking about nothing important.

The Russian eventually became quiet and put his head down and refused to smoke any more. He sat there for a minute, a worried look formed on his face. Emily wondered if he was thinking about sex.

"Will you excuse me?" he said, standing up. "I'll be right back." Emily watched him go and then stared at the TV and repeated, *I'll be right back*, trying to mimic his accent. The idea that he was going to walk in wearing some kind of pervert's outfit, leather, or a dress, or a diaper, crossed her mind. She wasn't too worried. He seemed all right. She was fucked-up herself but she could scream loud if she had to. She smoked from the pipe, stood up, and strained her ears, trying to listen for any sounds. Then, distracted, she put the pipe down and fixed her hair in the bathroom mirror.

Five minutes later he came back in. He walked the length of the room like he was preparing a speech, and then his hands went to his pants pockets and then up to his breast pocket. He pulled out some money.

"I said I'm not a prostitute."

"Oh, no, no—this? Shhh—no, I wanted to give you this as a gift. Just for coming here. Don't worry—I have so much money." The bills were shaking in his hand. "Friends," he said.

Emily took the money. She counted out ten twenty-dollar bills and laid them out on the bed in front of her. "I'm not gonna act in no porno movie, either—get all scandalous up in this hotel room—hell no." She seemed suddenly angry with him.

"Please," he said. "Just hanging around."

He had a smile on his face, but his eyes didn't look right. *Maybe he's just high*, she thought. "Well . . . stupid, Russian, cracker, punk," she said, and put the money into her front pocket. "Thank you." *Nothing's for free*, she thought.

"My wife's here," he said.

"I told you, I don't want to get into no freaky-deaky shit with you, man. Stop playing."

"No, please listen, she's here—"

"Hell no, motherfucker, please yourself."

"No, please, we are here, to *make* money," he said. He was visibly high. "We have a plan to make some. We are asking you if you want to help? To join us? You know, partner kind of thing?"

"Yeah, right," said Emily.

"It's the truth."

"Well, where is she?"

"She is in our room—not feeling, she's not feeling well." He put his hands up like he didn't know how to explain it. "Tomorrow we meet."

"How y'all gonna make this so-called money?" Emily asked.

"We have a plan, but I can't tell you it right now."

"Then how am I gonna decide?"

"There is no need to decide, here—now. You can stay in this room, for free, obviously. If you want to leave, you can leave." He turned his head and looked toward the door. "But if you leave, you can't come back."

"Y'all Mr. Mysterioso."

"I am," said the Russian. He looked dreadful.

"It's all good," she said. "I don't have anything better to do." The image of her boyfriend, Pierre, popped into her mind; he had been yelling at her, she could feel the bruises on her arm where he had shaken her. If she was going to leave him—and now, finally, maybe she was—she needed some money.

"We will pay you by the day until we decide if you should actually join us. Two hundred a day." His face looked like he was feeling stomach pains.

"You gonna interview me, or something?" she asked.

The Russian forced out a laugh and then asked, "Are you interested?"

"Shit, for two hundred, you could sign me up," she said.

The Russian smiled again. He looked a little unstable. "Oh, I nearly forgot," he said. He stood up and patted his pants and pulled out a prescription bottle and rattled it. "I have some pills for you—for us, to take."

"What kind of pills?"

He looked at the bottle. "Oak-see," he said. He opened the bottle and poured out a handful.

"You really trying to do your thing?" she said. She was drunk and high. She licked her lips. She did a self-assessment and found there was still pain inside of her that needed to be killed.

"Take them," he said.

"You gonna take 'em, too?"

"Of course. Come on, partners?"

"You take 'em first."

He took one, held it between his finger and thumb, put it in his mouth, grabbed his beer, took a sip, and swallowed.

"How many do you want?" he asked, his accent seeming to have grown along with his intoxication.

"How many you got? Just playing. Gimme three. What are they, twenties, thirties? Four's good."

She examined the pills: they were thirty milligrams, oxycodone, baby blue with a stamped *M*. The name on the prescription was "Valton Getty." She swallowed three with her beer and then wrapped the fourth in one of her new twenty-dollar bills and began crushing it on the table with her lighter. Then she unwrapped it, tapped it out onto the table, crushed it some more, rolled the bill into a straw, and snorted it quietly, like she didn't want to make a scene.

"Now we're talking," she said, rubbing around her nostrils with her fingers.

"Undoubtedly."

They small-talked. Emily got up and went to the bathroom. When she came back she noticed her beer had been moved; the label, when she left, had been facing her, and now it faced him. He had picked up her beer. Her thirst overwhelmed her caution and she drank.

The Russian stared at her for a moment as though lost in thought. Then he said, "And Emily, I am sorry, but we must ask for your phone." He walked over to her and held out his hand.

"Y'all getting all National Steal from Emily Day up in here?"

"You understand," he said, "our plans are big and good, but they're secret. No talking."

She handed him her phone.

"I'll take this, too," said the Russian, walking over to the hotel phone and unplugging it (bent over, his breathing heavy) from the wall.

"You tripping, though—that's on you, I ain't paying." *I can fight him*, she thought. *I could fight him. I could scream.*

"I will leave you now to think over this—how is it—everything. We should be able to make real money. Not hundreds, but thousands and thousands."

"A thousand thousand's a million," said Emily.

"Exactly," said the Russian, with the same sad face. He walked self-consciously to the door, said good night, and left her alone in the room.

Emily immediately thought about grabbing the crack (there was still some sitting on the nightstand), putting the beers in a pillowcase, calling a cab from the lobby, and heading back to the city. It would have been a good night. She walked around the room on her tiptoes, like she was trying not to wake anyone, and strained her ears again to listen, but she couldn't hear anything. She wanted to look outside, but for some reason she felt scared. She decided to sleep where she was and talk to the Russian and his so-called wife in the morning. It was a nice room, she had to admit, and the Russian did seem like a pretty big-time business partner; not like the regular nickel-and-dimers who came to her with propositions of shoplifting Similac or finding BART cards with leftover fares to turn in for cash.

Fuck Pierre, she thought. She had caught her boyfriend text messaging with a bitch named La La—talking about: U R the Light of my Life. *Hell no.* When she had confronted him he had started yelling at her, grabbing her arms, telling her not to look at his phone. Twenty minutes after that she stole two hundred dollars from the pocket of his jacket. Teach him to put his hands on her. It was her money now. Let his ass suffer. He had to learn his lesson just like anybody else.

She played the coincidences out in her head. She'd left the dirty Auburn Hotel, where they lived surrounded by convicts and drug addicts, and ended up here at this nice hotel, surrounded by what—businessmen? She'd taken two hundred from Pierre and gotten two hundred from the Russian. Four hundred dollars. Can't argue with that. She was on a roll. At this rate she'd be rich.

Her mind drifted. It was all a little bit of rude good luck. Get rude now, get lucky later. Something like that. Four hundred dollars was a lot of money. And she had pills and rocks and beers and some kind of new Russian associate and his wife. A thousand thousands was a million. Things were looking good. Things were getting better. *I'm sippin' on Coke and rum, I'm like so what I'm drunk, it's the freaking weekend baby, I'm 'bout to have me some fun.*

She thought about these things for a while and then fell asleep, fully dressed, on the bed, above the covers.

When Emily opened her eyes she saw a man and a woman standing above her and looking down. The woman had brown hair and bangs, round glasses, and thick eyebrows. Her lips were dark with lipstick. She appeared to be in her fifties or sixties. She was little and plump and seemed like someone's nice mother or aunt. She looked Arab or Jewish or something. The man was the Russian. Everything was hazy.

Emily had no idea where she was. The lights were on. The Russian looked familiar but she couldn't place him. She couldn't move. She felt paralyzed, but not in a bad way. She felt wonderfully paralyzed, warm and heavy. Her mind—which normally raced—was quiet.

The woman bent down near Emily's face, put her hand on Emily's forehead, and pushed it back slightly so she could look into her eyes. Emily coughed a weak cough. The woman checked the pulse on Emily's neck. Her hand was warm and Emily felt happy someone was taking care of her. The woman patted Emily's head like a child and spoke incomprehensibly to the Russian, who just stared down at Emily with a grave look on his face. Then they walked away from her bed toward the door. Emily followed them with her eyes. There was another man standing there. He was younger than the Russian and had a military-looking haircut and a severe face. His brow was swollen and he had beady eyes. They left the room and closed the door. Emily, numb and hot, fell back to sleep.

She woke up sometime later. It seemed dark outside. She felt drugged. The Russian was sitting in the armchair watching TV. He didn't notice her. She sort of remembered who he was now—she remembered a plan to make some money, but she couldn't remember the specifics. What was happening to her?

"What time is it?" she asked.

"What time is it," said the Russian in his accent. He looked all around him like he had forgotten where he was, too. "It is nine forty-five in the evening. You must have really needed the sleep."

"What'd you give me?"

"Nothing."

"What kinda pills?"

"Oh, those—I took those, too."

Emily did a mental inventory of her body to make sure she hadn't been raped. She felt like she hadn't.

"Well, they were serious," she slurred.

"Don't worry," said the Russian. He stood up, walked to the bureau, and came back with two hundred-dollar bills. Emily, still lying down, pushed the blanket off herself. She was so hot. She took the money without thinking. Her pants were still on and she put the cash in her pocket to go along with the two hundred from Pierre and the two hundred from last night; six hundred. *Good things come in threes*, she thought. She stayed flat on the bed and turned her head to look at the Russian. She felt incredibly foggy, but again, not in an unpleasant way. In her head she wanted to argue, she was used to fighting about everything, but her body wouldn't respond.

"Man, well, listen," said Emily, pushing herself up onto one of her elbows. "I'm feeling extra f'd up. Maybe I should just head back, you know, call it a night, all that stuff."

"It's your choice, but you have yet to hear us out."

"Well, quit stalling and talk," said Emily, rubbing her eyes.

"It's not time yet. Tomorrow. For now we just relax," he said flatly. He waved his hand at her like she was being unreasonable. He stood up, walked to the bureau, grabbed the crack pipe, and brought it to her in bed.

There was a big rock in it. She smoked it. She needed it. "Shit," she said, exhaling metallic-smelling smoke.

The Russian said he would be right back and left the room. Emily again considered leaving, but she felt so heavy. She also liked making two hundred dollars a day. She couldn't argue with that; money was money. She hit the pipe again. The room grew. Her head grew.

After a few minutes the Russian returned with a Styrofoam container of Vietnamese noodle soup. He gave it to her. She didn't feel hungry, but she sipped from the broth. He held up a beer like a caricature of a man tempting someone and shook a pack of cigarettes with his other hand and set them next to her. Then he made her drink some kind of sports drink. She was sitting up in the bed like a hospital patient.

They watched TV in the room for about fifteen minutes. Eventually the Russian stood up and walked over to Emily's bed and held out a pill.

"No, I'm good," said Emily.

"It's for you."

"I'm all good. They're too strong for me."

"It's medicine."

"Well, I don't need it."

"Take the pill," said the Russian with a hint of anger in his voice. "We need you to take them. Just one more night."

Emily took the pill in her clammy hand. She didn't like being bossed. If someone like Pierre or one of her old boyfriends saw her, they wouldn't have recognized her. She looked at the pill—another 30 mg of oxycodone—took it, and swallowed it indifferently with her beer.

"Emily, I don't know how to explain it, but I wish you could just do the things I ask," said the Russian. "Everything will be so much better if you do."

"Whatever," said Emily.

The Russian walked to the door. "Please," he said. He looked desperate. He left the room.

Emily picked up the pipe one more time and smoked from it. She told herself it wasn't because she needed it; more just to take all she could from the Russian. Maybe he was going to stop giving her money. *Take all I can from this motherfucker.*

She looked around the room: there was a bureau, a bed, a bookshelf, a chair, a desk, a TV stand, a TV, an end table, and a regular table with two chairs. How much could she get selling all these things on Market Street? At least thirty dollars for the TV.

She stared at the television for half an hour: detectives were driving around Los Angeles talking to rich people; a warmth flowed through her body, some kind of sinking and melting, the anger she was feeling eased, and then she fell back asleep.

She woke up again the next day. Her mouth was dry. The room was empty, quiet, and beige. She stared at a murky painting of a seashore. The television blared about the benefits of juicing.

She had to drag herself to the bathroom. Afterward, she lay down on the floor for a change of pace and drifted back to sleep.

At night she woke up and the Russian and the woman were standing over her again. They looked forty feet tall. Emily felt quiet and warm.

"Get up, dear," said the woman. She had an accent, too.

Emily rolled to her side and used her elbow to push herself halfway up. It took all her strength to sit. She felt embarrassed to be in such a state, sitting there on the floor, unable to even stand. She felt so heavy. Her tongue felt swollen in her mouth. She pulled the blanket on her lap and coughed.

The woman arranged a chair in front of Emily and sat down.

She said her name was Natalya, pointing at herself as though Emily didn't speak English. "Na-tal-ya," she said, sounding out the word. Then she said something foreign and the Russian nodded and left the room.

"Wake up, dear."

Emily rolled her head up and looked blankly at the woman. She had blacked out and now found herself off the floor and sitting in a soft chair. "We have been giving you too much medicine, haven't we?" said the woman, with a worried smile.

"You got me all in a state," mumbled Emily, sounding like she had just seen a dentist.

"That stupid man, he didn't listen to me. He gave you those pills," the woman said, shaking her head. "It was too much—what he gave you."

"That's what I been trying to say," said Emily, feeling as though she were trapped in the center of a conflict.

"We'll fix it," said the woman thoughtfully. "You'll do a different regimen tonight, one more suited for a girl like you." She brushed some hair from Emily's forehead and looked into her eyes. An itch spread on Emily's body like bug bites. She was too high to be concerned. She liked this woman. "We'll take care of you," said the woman. "We'll get you back in tip-top shape."

The woman sat down on the bed near the armchair. She put her hands on her own knees, like someone getting ready to talk business, and said, "You must be wondering what we want with you?"

"Yeah, I probably should just go."

"But you haven't been paid for today, my dear."

"That's all right, I just been sleeping anyway."

"Well," said the woman with a sigh, "let me give you your money for today."

"If you insist. But I don't know," Emily whispered.

The woman stood up and pulled out two hundred-dollar bills from her pants pocket; she snapped the bills tight on each end and held them out to Emily.

Emily's mind was saying *don't take it*. She didn't want to be indebted to these Russians. She said these things to herself, but she couldn't help it. Her hand reached out and took the two bills.

"Now I want you to shower," said the woman.

A shower would be nice. The woman pulled Emily up from the chair and walked her to the bathroom. Emily had to pause at the door. She forgot what she was doing.

Even standing took effort. The woman brushed past her and reached into the shower and turned it on. She looked back and smiled at Emily, tested the temperature of the water, and told her to get in.

She helped Emily pull her clothes off and guided her to the shower. Emily stood under the showerhead nearly asleep. The water, warm and high-pressured, made her feel clean. Her thoughts were soft and unfocused. Eventually, she became aware that she should turn the thing off.

"Put your new clothes on," called the woman from the other room. There was a shopping bag on the toilet. Inside it was a new navy blue tracksuit, a white T-shirt, some socks, a bra, and underwear. It took all her energy to get dressed. The clothes were clean and comfortable but the work made her head hurt. *They buying me hella stuff,* she thought, as she moved the money from her old pants to her new ones. She looked at herself in the mirror; her face looked slack and dumb.

When she came back out the woman looked her over, then walked to the table and returned with a little tube of cream. "For your face," she said. She smeared some cream around a sore under Emily's mouth. Emily was confused but resigned. A cool medicinal smell lifted her stomach.

"Now sit," said the woman. "I tell you, it is very simple what we want you to do. It is a simple case of identity theft. Listen to me. We plan on making nearly a million dollars, a third—thirty-three-point-three percent of which, of course, will go to you. This is not small business."

"Why me?" asked Emily.

"You look the part. You look exactly perfect for the part."

"What kind of identity theft?" mumbled Emily.

"Simple."

"Simple?"

Emily forced herself to focus: Money? Identity theft? Simple? She was too tired to figure out answers to any of it. The questions looped into her head and then floated out. It wasn't that her mind was confused, it just wasn't working very well. There was a humming in her ears. She fell asleep again.

She woke up a few times throughout the night, thought about trying to leave, and then fell back to sleep. At one point, she managed to check if the eight hundred dollars was still in her pocket. It was.

The next day she woke up alone. Her eyes scanned the room. It was clean. The carpet was oatmeal colored and the walls had vague stripes. She could go. There was nothing between her and the door. With effort, feeling heavy and dazed, she managed to get up and walk to it. It was locked, but just by the dead bolt. She turned the bolt and opened the door and looked outside. It was blindingly bright. *Nothing too much out there*, she thought. She closed and locked the door and lumbered over to the TV, turned it back on, went to the bed, and fell back to sleep.

Later the woman woke her by shaking her shoulder. She was with the Russian. He barely nodded at her. He was busy fussing with a small digital camera. Emily stared at him from the bed. His shoulders were slumped down and he seemed to be in a depressed mood. He needed a shave and he was wearing the same clothes as the first night. Had she underestimated him?

The woman made Emily sit up and began to brush her hair with a large plastic brush. She brushed and hummed to herself. Emily watched everything in a detached way. It was normal for someone to brush her hair. It was normal for a man to stand in her room with a camera in his hands. She couldn't stop what was happening.

"When are we gonna do this thing?" asked Emily.

"Yes, dear," said the woman.

Emily waited for an answer but it never came. It felt like the brush was making Emily's hair grow longer. Her head leaned in whichever direction the woman pulled. After a while the woman went to the mirror and brushed her own hair and then came back and put a little bit of powder on Emily's face. The Russian sat down on one of the chairs and watched television. The woman dabbed some kind of cover-up on Emily's chin, then poked her lips with a wine-colored lipstick and smeared it around with her finger. It was a strange way to do it. Her fingers smelled like cigarettes.

Emily nodded off. She woke up feeling the woman rubbing her face; she had taken a napkin and wet it and was cleaning something off of Emily's chin. Emily tried to shrug her off.

"There, there," said the woman.

The Russian said something Emily didn't understand—it must have meant he was ready because the woman smiled and pulled Emily out of bed. *This is the porno*, thought Emily. She tightened up.

The woman walked behind, her hands pushing Emily forward. She walked her to the wall, turned her around, and stepped to the side. Emily stood there swaying. She felt sick.

The Russian was speaking his weird language to the woman. He stood six feet from Emily. He lifted the camera to his eye and said, "Say cheese."

"Cheese."

The flash went off. The woman was standing behind the Russian, looking on like a mother.

"Say cheese," he said again.

"Cheese." Emily tried to look pretty the way she always did for pictures.

Another flash. "Perfect."

The Russian lowered the camera, looked at the display screen, and then looked at Emily for a moment. He seemed satisfied. He coughed and then put the camera into his pocket.

Emily woke up to find herself already awake. She was at the table, pushing ash and cigarette butts with her bare hand into an ashtray. The woman was watching her. Emily continued to clean the mess. She pushed as much as she could over the edge of the table into the ashtray and then looked at the trail of gray smudges on the brown table. Her hand and arm felt detached from her body. She was thirsty.

"Go wash your hands now, Emily," said the woman.

Emily stood up and turned toward the bathroom. She felt heavy and light. The room had turned even more orange, the greens in the furniture became blue, the carpet seemed to have grown significantly longer. Emily smiled as she took little steps to the bathroom. The floor pitched and heaved. She felt, in a pleasant way, like she was dreaming.

In the bathroom she rinsed her hands. She stared into the mirror for a few moments. She appeared to be a strange replica of herself.

"Emily," called the woman, "come back in here, dear."

Emily listened to the voice: "Emily . . . Emily . . . Emily."

She woke up. She was in bed. The woman was standing over her. "Emily, it's time to wake up. I have your money. Come on."

Emily, still lying flat on her back, took the money in her hand and crumpled it up. The woman watched her with a concerned face and then pointed at Emily's new pants, which were folded on the ground.

"Put it in there, with the rest of it."

Emily picked the pants up off the floor and put the money into the pocket with the other bills. She didn't bother counting it. She just stuffed it in. She was confused about why the new pants were on the ground and not on her. She looked at her own pants, which she was wearing again. They looked unfashionable: they were stretched and dirty.

The woman gestured toward the room: "We have to clean. It's getting dirty. I'll do it. Sit down. Clean the ashtray." Emily looked to where the woman was pointing. There was an overfilled ashtray on the table. She walked to it. "Put it in here," said the woman, holding open a large, black trash bag. Emily picked up the ashtray and poured it into the bag. The dust of the ashes moved up like smoke. Her mouth was dry.

It had been six days in the hotel now. Six days filled with sleep. When she wasn't sleeping, when she floated back up into the world, Emily was greeted by the Russian, the woman, or both.

"You need to start doing a little more work," said the woman at one point. "We're paying you!"

"What?" was all Emily could manage to say.

"Look," said the woman, pointing at the table. Emily looked and saw a Styrofoam container filled with food. "You're making a fucking mess," said the woman.

"That's not mine," said Emily.

"Come," said the woman. Emily stepped toward the table. The woman, her face made ugly with anger, stuck her fingers into the brown gravy, held them up for Emily to see, and then smeared the gravy across the table. "Clean it," she said, holding a bathroom towel out for her.

Emily stepped forward and cleaned the gravy with the towel. The woman lifted the container and dumped the remaining food onto the table. "Clean it," she said.

Emily began wiping at it with the towel, but the woman, her eyebrows raised, interrupted her by pointing at a trash can. Emily, feeling a strange disassociation with her own body, brought the trash can to the table, put the Styrofoam container into it, and then, with the towel, pushed in the mess of gravy and food off the table and into the trash. She then wiped up the remaining mess.

"See, good, not too hard, right?" said the woman. "A little work never killed anyone."

They fed her candy as a reward. They gave her Starbursts. The three of them, Emily and the woman and the Russian, would sit at the table and eat candy, piling wrappers in the center. They made her drink soup and eat slices of bread. The sore under Emily's mouth had healed. She was being taken care of. She slept.

The woman would stand over Emily's bed and—in a voice that was meant to sound comforting—sing Sinatra songs. She would sing *It had to be you,* her accent pronounced and her voice flat. *It had to be you.*

It was 11 a.m. The woman brought in another blue bag of clothes.

"Time to get dressed," she said, holding up a navy blue sweater. "Turtleneck—no, bra first, in the bathroom—bra, turtleneck, then sweater," said the woman, pushing Emily into the bathroom. The Russian sat at the table.

Emily, after what seemed like a long time, stepped out of the bathroom. She looked different in the new clothes. "How do I look?" she slurred.

"You look like an honest person," said the woman, taking Emily's shoulders in her hands and turning her side to side. "Drink this," said the woman, holding out a glass filled with cloudy water. "Medicine."

Emily drank it; bitterness spread from her tongue to her shoulders and ears. She tried to push it back but the woman forced the glass to her mouth and tipped it back. Emily drank.

The woman helped Emily pull on her shoes.

"How do you feel?"

"I'm feeling like a . . ." She searched her head, but there was nothing. She didn't know how she was feeling.

"Well, you look like a beautiful actress," said the woman. "And today is the day. No more waiting around. It's money time." She sang into Emily's ear, matching the words to the tune of the Sinatra song, "It's time to make money." Then she kissed Emily on both cheeks and clapped her hands at the Russian.

"Wake up, everyone," said the woman. "Emily, you need to smoke your little pipe, you need to wake up—today is the day—give her the pipe!" she yelled at the man. He brought the pipe and the woman held it up to Emily's mouth and lit it for her.

"Smoke it!"

Emily smoked it. She leaned her head sideways and held on to the woman's arms for balance. The woman put the pipe to her own mouth and pretended to smoke it herself. Then she handed it to the Russian, who after making a little show of shrugging his shoulders, smoked it in earnest. The woman held it back up to Emily's mouth and she smoked again.

They left the hotel. It was the first time Emily had been outside in a week. The light from the sun was white and Emily had to hold her left hand over her eyes. She walked arm and arm with the Russian, as though she were being helped across ice, back through the courtyard and out to the parking lot.

The woman went ahead of them and walked to a large, windowless white van. She pulled open the sliding door and waited for them. Her eyes and hair sparkled. When Emily and the Russian reached her, the woman stepped into the van, and then turned around and helped Emily climb in. She guided her down onto the bench seat just behind the driver's seat.

"I don't know if I'm ready for all this," said Emily.

"It's no problem, a withdrawal, walk in, walk out—voilà," said the woman, patting Emily's head and buckling her in.

Walk in, walk out? This lady tripping, thought Emily.

The woman showed Emily a pair of black leather gloves.

"I'm gonna wear your things?" asked Emily. Her mind was warped; she felt one step behind, she felt tangled up.

"Today you can do whatever you want," said the woman.

The Russian got into the driver's seat and started the van.

The woman took out a small flashlight and examined both of Emily's eyes, then touched her on the tip of her nose and buckled herself in. Emily sat with her chin resting against her chest. The van floated out of the parking lot. The hotel disappeared. "My whip float hard," said Emily.

They joined the other traffic on the 101 and started out for the city. Georgy, the younger, ugly man that Emily had noticed on the first night, followed behind in a gray sedan.

"Emily, listen to me," said the woman, "listen, listen—you can do anything in this entire world, you hear me. You are a beautiful, gifted, sweet thing. You are talented, and you will listen to me, and you will do just like I tell you. Okay?" The woman's perfume and lipstick were overpowering.

"Okay," said Emily.

They drove in silence for a bit and then, as though re-membering something, the woman said, "Emily, we have a slight change in plan." The Russian adjusted the rearview mirror and watched them through it.

"No problem," said Emily, bumping up and down with the road. She felt perfectly high. "No problemo."

"It will be so much easier now," said the woman. "You don't even need to talk to them—barely—you just go in and give the manager—she's a redhead—give her this phone." She held up a silver cell phone. "Give her the phone and we will talk with her. She's in it, too, Emily, she's a—a team member."

"She gets a third, too?" asked Emily.

"No," said the woman. "She gets a flat fee."

"What about the cameras?" asked Emily.

"We have it all worked out, your clothes, a disguise." The woman held up a black wig. "We have glasses, too. Everything is perfectly arranged—besides, please, it's a misdemeanor. Misdemeanor identity theft. You've done worse. We've done worse. We've all done worse."

The woman took Emily's hand in her own and rubbed it like she was checking to see if it was clammy or not. Then she checked Emily's forehead. Emily wanted to close her eyes and float.

"Shit is fucked-up," said Emily.

The Russian tilted his head to see.

"That's right," said the woman.

Emily relaxed her mouth and let her tongue hang out. She looked at the woman: black tracksuit; makeup. The whole thing seemed like a costume.

They were on the straight part of 101, passing the bay on the right and Brisbane on the left. A thick fog was coming in over the hills. Candlestick Park was coming up on one side. Emily thought about Pierre. He was a 49ers fan. She closed her eyes and a floating four-sided head, each side made of Pierre's face, appeared in her mind's eye, and said: "Like I always told you, the mouse plays the cat, and the cat watches in the crowd." She opened her eyes and turned to look at the woman next to her. She was looking at Emily in a concerned way. "I didn't say that," said Emily.

A small warning signal worked its way through the high into Emily's mind: for a moment it became clear to her that she was riding in a van next to a Russian woman on her way to withdraw a million dollars from a bank. Something didn't seem right about it. The moment of realization rose up like the bow of a ship and then disappeared.

They were back in the city now. Houses were packed in tight gray rows on all sides of the freeway. It felt, to Emily, like the van might fall on its side. She put her hand on the seat in front of her, opened her mouth like she was yawning, and tried to twist her head straight. They drove past the Alemany projects. Pierre's other girlfriend, La La, lived there. "Keep going," said Emily.

"Shh," said the woman, patting Emily on the hand and reaching for a black backpack on the floor. She pulled out a plastic water bottle, guided Emily's head back, and poured water into her mouth.

"Mmm," said Emily, smacking her lips. The water tasted like Kool-Aid.

What was she on? Whatever it was, it felt good. It didn't feel like anything she had felt before. She felt nauseous, but even that was okay; it grounded her. Otherwise she might just nod out. She tried to calculate the intensity of the high, but she couldn't. She was simply blasted.

They drove through the Sunset. A memory passed through Emily's mind: twelve years earlier, when she had first moved to the city, she used to take the train out to the beach with her friend Meagan. There was a boy named Salvador, who would sit at the bus stop in front of the hotel at Forty-Eighth and Judah and sell crystal meth, ten dollars for a tenth of a gram. He wore baggy jeans like a raver. He'd make them whisper how much they wanted, then they'd put the money into the coin slot of a pay phone, and he'd deposit the drugs and take the money. Then they'd walk up two blocks to the next shelter and sniff the bag. Then they'd walk all the way downtown from there. Years later, Meagan got cleaned up and found God. She got married to a man who strangled her in Stockton.

The van entered Golden Gate Park. The Russian said something to the woman; everything confused Emily, but she couldn't ask for clarification. She tried to imitate the woman's face. The Russian was speaking, but Emily couldn't understand what he was saying. He sounded concerned. He kept raising his hand.

"What the fuck is he saying?" asked Emily. Nobody answered her.

They drove into the Richmond District. Schools of cars passed here and there. The woman was directing the Russian on how to drive: "Turn right, turn right." The van drifted through the streets.

The Russian pulled the van over at Masonic and Euclid and turned the engine off. He and the woman were both speaking in Russian at the same time. They seemed angry. Emily, in an effort to calm them down, raised both of her hands up and dropped her chin, but they ignored her.

After a minute the Russian put on a white painter's hat and black sunglasses. He didn't seem happy. Emily had never seen him upset. The woman checked Emily's eyes again. She straightened out Emily's hair and made little clucking noises. Then she grabbed Emily's face with her hands and kissed her dryly on the lips.

The woman put on a white hat of her own and big black sunglasses. She pulled Emily's gloves tighter onto her hands.

"Okay, dear," said the woman, as she fit some kind of device into Emily's ear. She took out two cell phones and pressed buttons on both. "Testing, testing, one, two, three," she said into one of the phones, with the other one lifted to her ear. Emily watched as the woman plugged something into one of the phones and then placed it into Emily's sweater pocket. She noticed the woman's hands shaking as she buttoned the pocket closed.

"But I don't know what I'm supposed to do," said Emily.

"Just like I said," the woman answered.

The Russian was still talking. He looked in the rearview mirror and then looked at the one on the passenger side. Emily tried to roll her head back to look, too, but she couldn't. The van was moving again.

The woman produced a black doctor's bag from somewhere and set it down in front of Emily. The Russian would not stop talking.

The van continued up Masonic. Emily looked out her window toward downtown and felt some kind of recognition. She opened her mouth and stuck out her tongue in an effort to gain control of her face.

The van turned right onto Geary. Emily looked at the Lucky Penny diner. It looked like a circus.

"Safe, baby," said the woman again, reaching over Emily's head and turning the earpiece on. "Testing, you hear me?"

"Yep," said Emily. She could hear the woman in the earpiece.

The van pulled up a half a block east of the Palm-Geary branch of US Bank. The woman grabbed Emily's hands and said, "Emily, the time has come. Don't worry about anything. Much easier now. Just walk in and go to the manager's desk. As I told you, she is a redheaded woman—in fact she is Russian. She will be sitting out on the main floor. She's waiting for you. The redhead—remember, it's nothing. Very safe. They are waiting. You'll see her there. Just walk up and give her this phone—hand it to her." She handed Emily another silver cell phone and continued.

"Hold it in your hand. We will be monitoring you, and we will be talking to you on your earpiece. No problems." The words came at Emily like tires rolling down a hill; they were grouped, and moving in the same direction, but she couldn't put them together into something that made sense. Emily looked at the woman and saw sweat on her forehead.

The woman put a necklace with some kind of pendant over Emily's head and then put a black wig over her hair. *I already got black hair,* thought Emily. The woman was straightening out the wig and putting a pair of sunglasses onto Emily's face.

"There you go, honey. Just for show."

"You want me to rob them?" Emily managed to ask.

"Please, Emily, don't be silly," said the woman. "She is our business partner, this redhead—an associate. Just do this and you get your money and we drop you off back home free. You can start a new life. You know, bingo."

Then the woman lifted the black doctor's bag and handcuffed it to Emily's right hand. The bag was closed. Emily didn't understand its purpose.

"You want me to rob a bank?" said Emily. The words came out slow and stretched and floated around the van. She was looking down at the bag. It almost seemed funny.

"That's enough," said the woman, not loud, but directly into Emily's ear. She reached for Emily's seat belt and unfastened it. Then she grabbed both of Emily's wrists and pulled her up out of the seat.

"Now go," she said, with a little push to the small of Emily's back.

"Walk to the bank, Emily," said the voice in Emily's earpiece. The words swung her forward. She took a few steps toward the door.

The bank was a cube-shaped building decorated with flagstone and corrugated metal. Everything confused Emily. Her head, under the wig, led the way.

"The door, Emily, easy," said the woman's voice in her ear. Emily squinted at the entrance like a drunk. Her earpiece was silent. She opened the door of the bank and dragged herself in.

Customers slouched in a line. Behind the windows women worked quietly, their heads shaking in unison. Nobody appeared to notice Emily as she stepped into the room.

"Walk to the redhead."

Emily squinted through her sunglasses. There was a row of desks set off on the opposite side of the room from the tellers; two of the desks were empty, but at the third a red-headed woman sat typing at a computer. Emily lifted her hand toward the woman and then staggered forward. The woman's hair was a bright red beacon.

"Give her the phone," said the voice in Emily's ear.

Emily stopped at the desk and stared down at the redhead, who looked up nervously.

"Give her the phone from your hand!"

Emily had forgotten the phone. She had forgotten the bag attached to her arm, had forgotten her clothes, her wig, everything. Her attention was on the room and how it was expanding and contracting with every breath she took.

"Tell her to listen to it."

"Here," said Emily. She held out the phone.

"I'm sorry, I don't understand?" said the redhead. Her face was constricted.

Emily was in a cloud. Sweat appeared on her face like she was pulling moisture from the air.

A phone on the redhead's desk rang. The redhead ignored it. Emily was confused. She didn't know what to do. She opened the phone she was holding for the redhead and spoke into it.

"Hello?"

"Emily, kindly give her the phone!" said the voice on the other end. Emily heard it on the phone and a split second later in her earpiece, which only added to her confusion. She was becoming flustered. She held out the phone and stared at it.

"The phone!"

She held it out again and finally the redhead took it from her, put it to her ear, and said something into it.

"Emily, take the black bag you have on your wrist and show it to her, dear. She is fine—good, just open it and show it to her."

Emily looked down at the doctor's bag attached to her wrist. She raised it up and struggled to open it. She looked at the redhead. The redhead was staring at Emily and listening to the silver cell phone. She looked scared; her mouth was open. Her face looked insulted. She was speaking into the phone.

"Emily, show her the bag!"

"Show me the bag!" hissed the redhead without moving her lips.

Was this the identity theft? With her right hand Emily unclipped the doctor's bag and held it open: there were wires coming out of a big square of gray clay. An electronic face at the top of the contraption blinked, red-green, red-green. Even in her state, Emily could tell what it was.

She looked to the redhead for advice. The redhead's face had blanched white; pink blotches were appearing on her neck and chest. Emily's earpiece was silent.

"I don't know," said Emily to nobody in particular. The room seemed to darken.

"Emily, sit down at the desk."

Emily slumped down into a chair. She tried to pull the bag off her wrist, but she couldn't. She turned the bag over and tried to shake the bomb out of it, but it was attached to the bag. She thought about pulling the wires out, but she became scared it would explode. She turned and looked at the door. She wanted to run. She hadn't noticed the security guard standing by the entrance, right where she had come in. He was an old Chinese man, rocking on his feet. He looked at Emily for a moment, then looked away. He seemed to be whistling.

The redhead was speaking heatedly into the phone. Emily leaned on the desk in front of her; she wanted to put her head down and sleep, throw up, anything. She could hear yelling coming from the cell phone.

"I thought y'all were supposed to be friends," Emily murmured to the redhead.

"Okay," the redhead said into the phone.

"Emily, walk with her."

The redhead got up. Emily got up.

"Can you hear me?" Emily asked.

"Yes," came the woman's voice from the earpiece.

"What the fuck?" asked Emily.

"Shut up," said the woman. *"Walk with her—simple."*

"You're really fuckin' me up," said Emily.

"The point is to act normal."

The redhead was walking sideways in front of Emily like she didn't want to turn her back on her. She was staring at Emily's chest. Emily looked down: in the middle of her torso, hanging flat from the gold chain, was what looked like a small camera. She stopped walking and turned the camera up toward her own face.

"Emily, please," came the voice in her ear.

She let the camera fall back flat against her chest and looked up. The redhead was standing a few feet from her with both of her hands up as though she were holding a newspaper. Tears were streaming down her face; her eye makeup was smearing. Emily reached out to console her and the redhead flinched backward.

"Emily, please, walk with her."

The redhead continued her crab-walk toward the bullet-proof-windowed section of the bank. She punched in a code and opened the section's outermost door. Emily followed her through it.

The three female bank tellers turned and stared at Emily with bored, questioning looks. The customers continued waiting and filling out forms. The redhead gestured for the tellers to look away by waving her hand once in a downward swipe and just like that, the three tellers' heads swung forward in unison.

The Russian sat in the driver's seat of the van and waited. Cars and buses drove past in slow motion. People walked east and west on Geary.

The woman sat behind the Russian and spoke into her phone, but the Russian couldn't understand the words anymore. He had stopped listening. His mouth was so dry. He wanted to smoke crack. He wanted to run away.

He looked across the street. Georgy was parked on the other side of Geary. He was wearing sunglasses but he appeared to be staring directly back at him. *As ugly as a* chort, thought the Russian.

A police car rolled past. A car horn blared continuously. The woman wouldn't stop talking. Life was unbearable.

The redhead was gesturing for Emily to follow her. A young, dough-faced man wearing a tie had materialized from somewhere and now walked within touching distance of Emily. He seemed scared. "Problem at the bank," Emily mumbled to him. She was so thirsty. The room had suddenly grown loud. Emily couldn't tell what was happening, but nobody seemed to be panicking. The redhead was standing in front of a large circular vault door in the back of the room. The vault was already open, but there was a jail-bar door locked shut within it. The redhead fumbled with an electronic keypad and opened the inner door.

"Stay close to her."

Emily walked into the vault. Her ears were humming. "I'm in," she said. She turned to the redhead, who was lifting a tan canvas bag that looked like a mailman's sack. Emily reached out for it and almost fell down from the weight.

"Lift it and walk with her."

"Leave now!" said the redhead.

The redhead helped put the strap over Emily's shoulder. Emily let her do this.

"Keep walking, please don't do anything," said the redhead. *Foreigner*, thought Emily.

The three tellers turned again, staring. There was an older woman customer who was looking at them, as well. She held her head at an angle like a dog, her mouth gaped open.

The redhead's hand was on Emily's back, forcing her out of the banker's room and into the main lobby. The fluorescent lights were making all the faces look strange. The weight of the bag on Emily's shoulder, combined with the awkwardness of the one cuffed to her arm, was almost too much. Emily glanced at a TV monitor and saw herself—wearing the wig and glasses—on the screen.

She could smell the redhead's perfume, and feel the woman's hand hot on her back. The old Chinese guard was watching them with a shy, confused smile. He held the door open for Emily.

A gust of cool air met her as she stepped back out onto Geary Boulevard.

She looked across the street at a construction site and stood there with the bag over her shoulder like someone waiting to be picked up at the airport. She nearly nodded off then; her eyes closed for a moment. The van inched up in front of her.

The side door of the van coughed and slid open. The woman beckoned for her to come in. Emily stood frozen. The Russian was looking at her. Inside Emily's head, unthinkable thoughts were forming: *They want to kill me.* It became clear. They wanted to kill her and take the money.

Emily stepped backward, stumbled toward the bank, leaned into the door, and went back in. The redhead was standing at her desk with a phone in her hand. She looked terrified. The customers shrank away from Emily toward the back.

Emily stepped to the security guard, who was still near the door. He had an angry look on his face. His gun was already in his hand, and he rattled it at her. Emily lifted the doctor's bag toward him.

"Give me the gun!" Emily yelled.

"Give her the gun!" yelled the redhead.

"Come back out," said the woman in the earpiece. Emily brushed the thing off her ear like she would an insect and stepped on it. She took the phone from her sweater pocket and threw it to the ground. The bank tellers were cowering behind the windows with their hands over their mouths.

"Give her the gun!" yelled the redhead, and then, more calmly, in her thick accent, she said, "Daniel, please, give her your gun, I beg you."

The guard, ten feet from Emily, slowly lowered his gun, put it on the floor, and with his foot, sent it sliding over to her. Then he stood there with his knees bent and his arms raised. Emily wobbled over to the gun and lifted it. She was desperately tired and high. She struggled to get the big bag off her shoulder and set it down on the ground.

"You, go!" she said to the guard, waving him out with the gun. She turned toward the customers and they fell back farther. The camera on her neck caught her attention; she pulled it over her wig and dropped it to the ground. Her wig needed fixing. Her glasses were crooked. The tiredness was all she could feel. She wanted to lie down on the bank floor and sleep. With her left hand, the one cuffed to the doctor's bag, she pinched her neck as hard as she could. She didn't make herself bleed, but it hurt enough to wake her.

The street. The van was still sitting there. She waited and the van waited. The police were on their way.

"You," she said to the guard again. He was still standing by the door. "Go out there."

"Please, I don't want trouble," he said.

"Go!" She held the gun on him.

Crouching down, with his hands in the air, he shook his head at her. "My family," he said.

Emily raised the gun at him again. It felt as heavy as a sledgehammer. He grabbed the front door, swung it open, and stepped out.

The van's engine roared, its tires squealed, and it took off down Geary. The guard ran in the opposite direction.

Emily turned and lifted the bag onto her shoulder, stumbling a few steps to her right. She nearly fell over. She looked at the redhead, the tellers, and the customers; all of them were staring at her, panicked. "Fuck you all, and don't follow me," she said, and stumbled back out onto the street.

The bag felt so heavy she had to drag it. Looking over her shoulder, she headed west toward Palm Avenue; at some point she pulled off the black wig and stuffed it into the bag with the bomb. The glasses and gun she put on top. *Fuck you, bomb.* She tried again to empty the bag of the bomb by shaking it, but only the gun fell out, clanking down on the sidewalk. *Fuck you.* The sound of sirens was growing in the distance. She stuffed the gun back into the bag.

She crossed Geary. Six lanes of endless traffic.

The white van, apparently, had circled the block; now it was coming back down Geary. She stood behind a car looking dumbly at it. It raced past her, turned left against traffic, and was gone again.

Two police cars blared to a stop twenty feet from the bank. Four cops jumped out, then hid behind their cars with guns pointed at the front door. Emily watched from a block down. All of this was being filtered through her drugged mind. Her mind was a tunnel.

Her face felt epileptic. She got to Arguello Boulevard, where a crowd of people waited for the bus. The sound of sirens and traffic was everywhere. People were stepping around Emily to try to see what the commotion was at the bank. They jostled her. She could smell food on them.

A bus pulled up, and she joined a river of people moving toward the door. Her head hurt, like her brain was being crushed in a vise. She was sweating; her stomach burned. The MUNI driver stared at her as she climbed onto the bus.

"Can I have a ride?" Emily drawled.

The driver turned away from her. She walked a few rows down as the bus pulled back into traffic.

She fell into a seat somewhere in the middle, put the bag from the bank on her lap, and put the smaller bag with the gun and bomb on top of that. She dropped her head on top of it all and lost consciousness.

"Wake up, lady. Hello? Lady?"

Emily woke to see a Chinese man in a brown uniform standing over her. The bus lights were on; it was pitch black outside, and Emily was utterly confused about where she was. The lights made it seem like she was in jail, or a hospital. It was a bus, she could see that now, but what bus? What city? Where was she?

Her mouth was dry, her tongue swollen. Her eyes were not working properly. There were no other passengers on board.

"Come on, lady. End of the line."

She pushed herself up to her feet. Her legs and back felt like she had slept in a box. She held the big bag to her chest, not even knowing what was inside, but instinctively protecting her property. The bag with the bomb hung from her left hand, and she weakly tried to shake it loose. *What are these bags?*

"Come on, ma'am."

"Argh you mmm," said Emily, dragging herself toward the front. She grabbed the handrail at the exit and lowered herself backward like an old woman. She felt grossly hungover. What had she done?

The driver pulled off a transfer and held it out to her, but she didn't understand the meaning of the gesture. "Out din it," said Emily, trying to thank him.

She didn't know it, but she was outside the VA hospital in the Richmond District, near Ocean Beach. There were three empty buses there, and no people.

Her ability to distinguish things was limited to light versus dark. She needed dark. There was an area of shade about fifty yards from the bus.

A park with trees. A dark park with trees and dirt and no light. She staggered that way and fell to the ground.

2

"Where we going?" asked Trammell. Normally, they drove their unmarked police car straight up Sixth Street to the Tenderloin and then over to the Fillmore, but today, Elias steered them onto the Harrison Street on-ramp and up over the city, above the fray, toward the Octavia Street exit.

"Gotta take a look at that bank real quick."

"What bank?"

"The one that got robbed."

"Oh, you trying to get all *extra credit* now," said Trammell. "I see." He rested his head back on the headrest and closed his eyes. He knew better than to question Elias.

They pulled up to the bank and parked in the exact spot where the white van had waited for Emily. Trammell sank lower into his seat and stared straight ahead.

Elias cut the engine and sat there tapping on the steering wheel, trying to think of something to say, but there was nothing. He wanted to make some kind of joke about stopping here, he wanted to volley something back at Trammell's suggestion of extra credit, but nothing was coming to him.

"Do what you gotta do," said Trammell, yawning.

Elias got out and walked to the door of the bank, the arches of his feet aching as he went. He shaded the sunlight at the window so he could look in. The door was unlocked, the bank was open, people were inside. He just wanted to see it. He wanted to match an image to his imagination, and here it was. His partner Trammell watched him from the car.

Elias turned around and looked up and down Geary. He closed his eyes and smelled at the air with his nose. *How could she just walk in and walk out like that?* A 38 Geary bus drove by on the opposite side of the street.

The kids in the Fillmore had given Elias the name "Plastic Face." They called him that because he had a way of setting his face into a mask of fake toughness. He hated the name. The name had spread from the Fillmore. Even his fellow cops were calling him Plastic Face.

Elias was wearing a gray hooded sweatshirt, a black Giants hat, some blue jeans, and a pair of skateboard shoes that shouldn't have been worn by a man in his forties. His trapezius muscles, overdeveloped by hours in the gym, gave his body a hunched look. He walked with his arms held out to the side.

Elias stared at the bank and wondered where his life had veered off track. When did he start feeling so desperate? He stared at the bank and wondered how a woman could get up the nerve to rob it.

"You ready?" called out Trammell through the window.

Elias, startled, turned. "Yep, ready," he said, and walked back to the car. *Ready, ready, ready.*

*   *   *

Earlier that morning Elias had received a letter from his bank: final notice on foreclosure. He hadn't told his wife, Julie, about the foreclosure. He had hidden every notice they received. He knew that the trickle of hate that had been dripping in her would turn into an outright flood if she found out. Julie had wanted her mother to move in with them. If Elias lost the house it would affect not just him, but their entire family. It had been his idea to move from their cheaper house in Hayward to this new one in San Mateo. He had insisted on it. He had also insisted, without her permission or knowledge, on investing all eighty-five thousand dollars of their savings into an absolute sure thing, a restaurant near the ballpark, which went belly-up within months. Julie, finding out that she was pregnant, had decided she wanted to quit her job. Now—because he had been attempting to plug the holes in his sinking ship by moving money and credit around, even sinking so low that he had begun to bet (and lose) on football games—the mortgage had gone unpaid, the broker had been ignored, and they were about to lose their house.

Elias had met Julie eleven years ago. They'd met through an online dating site. Julie, having moved to California from Ohio, at first found Elias, and the fact of him being a cop, kind of exciting. The excitement had faded. Elias had watched it fade, and now he was convinced that the only thing that had kept her from breaking up with him had been a steady string of promises: first the engagement, then marriage, then home purchases, and now a baby.

Elias was born in Daly City, but his family—his parents
and two older sisters—had moved to San Mateo when he
was eight years old. His father, a man physically defined by
the bags under his eyes, had worked as an engineer for Pacific
Gas and Electric; Elias traced back some of his desire to become a policeman to the love of his father's blue uniform.
His mother had been an accountant. Elias, had he been
pressed to think of her defining physical feature, would
have thought of her skinniness, and her legs, and how they
were always bruised. His mother was Irish, and Elias took
more after her than he did his Portuguese-American father.
Elias's two older sisters got the dark genes; they looked
Mexican. They had large breasts, they were grumpy, and
with their grumpiness they'd dominated Elias's childhood
home.

One of Elias's only girlfriends, a girl named Sonya (the
one that got away), had a brother who worked as a cop in
Oakland, and it was this man—with his plain clothes, his
strutting, his gun and his badge—who had truly made Elias
want to become a police officer. Still, it wasn't until four
years after having been dumped by Sonya that he finally got
around to joining the SFPD. The truth of the matter was,
he would have never joined had it not been for a friend of
his who signed them both up. That friend, a man named
Gerraldo Costello, a man he worked with at Sam Goody's, a
loud friend, prone to making loud speeches, had twisted his
ankle the very first week of the academy and never returned.
Elias was twenty-six years old when he joined.

Now, fifteen years later, he was a member of the SFPD
Gang Task Force.

That morning, at roll call, Sergeant Fleming had given an initial briefing to the men about the bank robbery. "So, beat the bushes on the Asian gangs," said the sergeant. "You never know."

The news of the robbery had made the top of Elias's ears burn. It made his stomach hurt. He was hit with a wave of envy. He became lost in a reverie thinking about it until he was interrupted by the sound of the other cops clapping and laughing about something the sergeant had said.

After the morning briefing Elias had walked straight down the hall from the Gang Task Force's office to the Robbery Division. "Hello?" he called out at the abandoned front desk, his voice sounding weaker than he wanted it to. A low-grade dread began simmering in his gut. Much later, after everything had happened, he would wonder why he had ever even gone there, and he would mark this moment as the beginning of the end.

"There he is!" said a short and stocky inspector named Delarosa, stepping to the desk with his arms crossed in front of him. "Officer Plastic Face in the flesh." This was exactly the kind of interaction Elias didn't want to have.

"Fuck you," said Elias, searching for a comeback and not finding one. He muttered "Delarosa" under his breath. *Delarosa. Delarosa.*

"Jesus, Leo, I'm just playing with you. But seriously, why's your face all red?"

Elias ignored him. He could feel the color spreading. He did what he always did in this kind of situation, bull forward: "Fleming was just telling us about that Richmond bank job," he said, scratching at the space above his lip, his forehead tilted forward. He gave the desk a little two-handed thump in an effort to project casualness.

"Big balls on that broad," said Delarosa, shaking his head.

"Who's working it?"

"They got Peed and—"

"Peed and Hefling?" interrupted Elias. *Calm down*, he thought, *Jesus, calm down*.

"Yeah, you should of seen him—Peed comes in here last night saying it's an inside job, it's an inside job. Anyway, the feds are on it." Delarosa leaned over the counter conspiratorially and continued talking: "You know how fuckin' Peed gets all stressed—he's going on and on about how some Russian worker at the bank took some phone call and kinda played the whole thing up."

Elias looked down at his own hand resting on the desk and saw wrinkles he had never seen before. "Russian?" he asked.

Delarosa nodded. "Peed's all, 'Open and shut.'"

"Well I guess it's not an Asian gang," said Elias. He was an actor, and these were his lines. He breathed in deep and breathed out shallow. He already wanted to drink.

"Who the fuck knows—last I checked, Russia was Asia. But Peed gets all worked up 'cause already there's some bank VP telling him why it's not an inside job, this and that, insurance and all, blah, blah, blah. Anyway, some chick, huh?"

"Un-freaking-believable," said Elias, noting to himself that that didn't sound the way he wanted it to; it sounded like something a high school student might say. "Some chick," he tried, but this felt fake, too. Elias shook his head, and then asked, "Listen, can you forward me the report so we can work up the gang angle?" He was struggling. His mouth was struggling. His forehead was tense. His hand went to his back pocket and unconsciously patted the foreclosure letter that he had earlier stuffed there.

"Of course, sweetheart. Anything else?"

"Nope, thanks, brother."

Thanks, brother. Thanks, brother. Thanks, brother.

He still was repeating, *Thanks, brother* in his head as he and Trammell drove away from the bank and headed toward the Eddy Rock projects. The clock on the dashboard said 10:20 a.m. Elias counted the hours until lunch, when he would be able to sneak away from Trammell long enough to drink some wine. He needed it. He told himself the drinking was going to last just this week; he would go back to being sober as soon as the house business was figured out. The wine was stashed in the trunk, capped up in a Gatorade bottle. White wine, he was convinced, didn't smell as bad as anything else so long as you kept eating oranges all day.

The next day Elias went back to the robbery detail to get the report. A grumpy inspector he didn't know disappeared to the back and then reappeared with a copy of it. He didn't bother asking why Elias wanted it. There was a yellow Post-it note with Elias's name on it stuck on the first page. Elias stepped back out into the hallway, folded the report, and stuffed it in the front of his waistband. He looked over his shoulder as he walked: nobody was following him.

In the men's bathroom he closed himself into a stall, sat down on the toilet, and read the first few pages of the report.

All they had given him was the initial incident report—no witness statements, no inspector's chronology, no pictures, nothing. If he went back and asked, the inspector at the counter would probably say, "Ask Peed for those."

Elias looked at the pages. There were fifteen witnesses in the bank at the time of the robbery. Which one was the Russian who took the phone call? Right at the top, the first witness listed had a Russian-sounding name: Rada Harkov. She was forty-two years old. Home address refused. Home phone refused. California driver's license number D23539401. He jotted down her CDL and DOB into his notepad. She appeared to be the only Russian person of interest.

The narrative was written by an officer named Danzig:

ON THE ABOVE DATE AND TIME DISPATCH SENT MYSELF AND OFC CHEUNG #430 (3H11D) TO 3550 GEARY BLVD ON AN "A" PRIORITY CALL OF A BANK ROBBERY IN PROGRESS. AS I APPROACHED THE CORNER OF GEARY AND JORDAN I SAW A SECURITY GUARD (V/R-3) WONG RUNNING E/B GEARY AWAY FROM THE BANK. (V/R-3) WONG WAS POINTING AT THE ENTRANCE OF THE BANK. MYSELF AND OFC CHEUNG CONTINUED TO THE BANK AND EXITED OUR MARKED PATROL VEHICLE. FEARING THAT (S-1) WAS STILL IN THE BANK WE PULLED OUR SERVICE WEAPONS AND SET UP A PERIMETER IN FRONT OF THE ENTRANCE. OFC DANDLES #1422 AND OFC PAN #128 (3H01D) ARRIVED AND ALSO SET UP A

DEFENSIVE PERIMETER AT THE FRONT OF THE BANK. NUMEROUS SFPD UNITS RESPONDED ON SCENE TO ASSIST.

AFTER APPROXIMATELY TWO MINUTES WHILE ATTEMPTING TO COMMUNICATE WITH DISPATCH (V/R-1) HARKOV EXITED THE FRONT DOOR WITH HER HANDS RAISED IN THE AIR. HARKOV WAS YELLING THAT SHE WAS THE MANAGER. OFC CHEUNG PULLED HARKOV SAFELY AWAY FROM THE DOOR. HARKOV TOLD OFC CHEUNG THAT (S/1) UNKNOWN FEMALE, WHITE OR HISPANIC, UNKNOWN AGE, 5'2"–5'5", BLACK HAIR, SLIM, WEARING BLACK OR BLUE SWEATER AND DARK PANTS HAD LEFT THE AREA HEADED IN AN UNKNOWN DIRECTION. RESPONDING OFFICERS CHECKED THE PREMISES AND MADE SURE NOBODY WAS INJURED AND BROADCAST FURTHER SUSPECT INFORMATION TO DISPATCH.

(V/R-1) HARKOV FURTHER STATED THAT (S/1) MAY HAVE BEEN PICKED UP IN AN UNKNOWN WHITE VAN. I IMMEDIATELY ASKED IF ANYBODY WAS INJURED AND NEEDED MEDICAL ATTENTION. (V/R-1) HARKOV SAID THEY WERE SHAKEN UP BUT NOT INJURED. I BEGAN ASKING (V/R-1) HARKOV WHAT OCCURRED. HARKOV STATED SHE IS THE MANAGER OF THE BANK. TODAY (S/1) UNKNOWN FEMALE ENTERED THE BANK AND APPROACHED HARKOV AT HER DESK WHICH IS SITUATED IN THE MAIN LOBBY OF THE BANK. (S/1) HANDED HARKOV AN UNKNOWN

CELLULAR PHONE. HARKOV SPOKE INTO THE PHONE THINKING (S/1) NEEDED TRANSLATION HELP. HAVKOV STATED THAT (S/2) UNKNOWN FEMALE SPOKE ON THE PHONE AND TOLD HARKOV THAT (S/1) WAS CARRYING A BOMB. HARKOV STATED THAT (S/2) SPOKE IN ENGLISH WITH NO APPARENT ACCENT. (S/1) AT THAT POINT SHOWED HARKOV HER BAG AND HARKOV DID SEE WHAT SHE BELIEVED TO BE A BOMB.

(V/R-1) HARKOV SAID (S/2) TOLD HER ON THE PHONE TO TAKE (S/1) TO THE VAULT AND GIVE HER THE BAG WAITING FOR PICKUP. HARKOV TOLD ME THAT THERE WAS A BAG CONTAINING APPROXIMATELY $880,000 WAITING TO BE PICKED UP FOR TRANSPORTATION THAT DAY. HARKOV FURTHER STATED THAT ONLY SHE HAD THE ELECTRONIC COMBINATION TO THE VAULT. HARKOV SAID SHE FEARED FOR HER LIFE. SHE TOOK (S/1) TO THE VAULT AND DID AS SHE WAS TOLD. HARKOV THEN WALKED (S/1) TO THE DOOR OF THE BANK. (S/1) STEPPED OUT OF THE BANK TO GEARY BLVD AND THEN RETURNED INSIDE FOR AN UNKNOWN REASON. (S/1) THEN DEMANDED THAT (V/R-3) WONG, SECURITY GUARD OF THE BANK, GIVE HER HIS GUN. HARKOV STATED THAT SHE TOLD WONG TO DO SO BECAUSE SHE WAS IN FEAR OF HER LIFE AND EVERYONE INSIDE THE BANK'S LIFE. (V/R-3) WONG GAVE (S/1) HIS GUN AND (S/1) EXITED THE BANK AND LEFT IN AN UNKNOWN DIRECTION.

5J13 INSP. PEED #1911 OF THE ROBBERY DETAIL
ARRIVED ON SCENE AND TOOK CHARGE OF THE
INVESTIGATION. HE REQUESTED THAT C.S.I. RE-
SPOND TO THE SCENE TO SEARCH FOR POSSIBLE
PHYSICAL EVIDENCE LEFT BY THE SUSPECTS.
5L15 INSP. PAILLE #303 ARRIVED AND BEGAN TO
PROCESS THE SCENE. OFC DENNY #806 BEGAN
A CRIME SCENE LOG. ROBBERY ABATEMENT
UNITS RESPONDED TO THE IMMEDIATE AREA
TO SEARCH FOR THE SUSPECTS. 5J200 LT. KOLTU-
NIAK OF ROBBERY ALSO ARRIVED AT THE SCENE.
    (V/R-1) HARKOV WAS GIVEN A VICTIM OF VIO-
LENT CRIME NOTIFICATION AND AN SFPD 105
FORM WITH THE CASE NUMBER, AS WERE THE
OTHER VICTIMS (V/R-1 - V/R18).

Blah, blah, blah, thought Elias. He had read enough.
Rada Harkov was in on it; he didn't need Inspector Peed or
Delarosa to point that out. He stepped out of the stall and
rinsed his face at the sink. The skin around his nose was red
with rosacea. His armpits were visibly wet.

He went back into the Gang Task Force office, sat down
at his desk, and punched Rada Harkov's name into his
CLETS computer. No record. No tickets. Nothing. He
picked up his telephone, looked around to make sure nobody was listening, and dialed the California DMV's law
enforcement hotline. He got her address and asked that a
photo be mailed to him.

Harkov's last known address, as of September 10, 2008,
was 417 Poplar Street, San Bruno. He looked at the house

on Google. He could almost see right in the window. It was near the cemetery.

Elias called Trammell on his cell phone and told him that he was ready to go.

That night, when their shift ended, Elias drove out to Rada Harkov's San Bruno address. He parked a few houses down and stared at her front door. San Bruno was a suburb; the houses had small lawns, and there were plenty of open parking spots.

The neighborhood was quiet. The fog had rolled in. The lights of Rada Harkov's house were on, but the shades were drawn. The outside walls, Elias noticed, needed cleaning.

A neighbor walked by with a dog. Elias, aware that a man speaking on cell phone draws less attention than a man sitting silently in a car, opened his phone and put it to his ear. "I know, honey," he said. "No you listen. Listen to me, please. I didn't say that."

He sat in the dark. His mind drifted. He thought about Trammell. Trammell had it so easy. He was everything that Elias was not: twenty-eight years old (Elias was forty-two); from Los Angeles (Elias was from San Mateo); laid-back, quick-minded, and handsome. Where Elias was soft, Trammell was fit. Elias was white, Trammell was black. Trammell moved easily through life. People liked him. All kinds of people liked him. And girls, too—female cops were always asking him out. They would do it right in front of Elias.

Elias's first partner, back when he had just joined the force, had been a red-faced Irish cop, named Gary Sheehan.

Sheehan was loud. He was from San Francisco. He knew everybody. He must have only been about forty-five at the time, but he seemed older. His sideburns were cut high, like a boy. His stomach was shaped like a basketball.

Elias was so nervous back then. He was scared of almost everything. Not just the violence and the action; he was scared of the other cops, too. They were so confident. So urban. He hadn't hung out with many black guys, and here it seemed that everyone was black; even the Chinese cops seemed black. Even Sheehan seemed black. Everyone had loud voices. They walked around like cowboys.

There was one week, early in Elias's career, that was worse than all the others. He was still riding with Sheehan. The week started with a call for a medical emergency. They arrived at the scene before the paramedics. The house was occupied by a Mexican family. A little baby was lying on the floor. Its diaper had loosened and rested under its body. For one absurd second, Elias thought the loose diaper was the issue. The mother was crying and listening to the baby's chest. There was a purple bruise running diagonally down the baby's neck. Later, they learned the baby had wedged its head into the side of the crib and had accidentally hung itself.

The room, crowded and filled with shouting, seemed too small to hold all the people. Sheehan took over. He was so focused. He cleared the room, began checking the baby, gave it mouth-to-mouth. Elias remembered feeling useless. He stood behind Sheehan and prayed the ambulance would show up. Eventually, he ran outside; it was too much. He pretended he had gone out to wave the paramedics in, but the truth was, he just couldn't take it. He threw up between parked cars on the street.

The very next night there had been a shooting. There was a young black kid, probably about fourteen years old, who had been shot. They found him on the ground at the corner of Sargent and Ralston streets. Nobody else was around. The kid was on his back, his arms wide open like he had been boasting about something. He was wearing a T-shirt that showed a smiling Ronald McDonald. The right side of the kid's face was crushed in. His left eye was white and open, but his right eye was a red mess. There was bone and brain on the street next to his head.

The day after that, Elias had come into the locker room to change into his uniform before shift. He'd heard Sheehan talking to three other cops in the locker room. He didn't hear everything Sheehan said, but he distinctly heard the words *Elias* and *faggot* followed by laughter.

This was shortly before Elias's promotion out of the Ingleside District and into the Gang Task Force. He had been at Ingleside for six years. Most of that time he'd been Sheehan's partner. Sheehan would drink almost every day. He didn't even try to hide it; he'd drink on duty, in uniform. Occasionally, he'd convince Elias to join him.

There was other trouble, too. Sheehan had been taking payments from a Plymouth Street crack dealer. It wasn't much, just a hundred every week. He told the dealer he'd keep the other cops away, but he never actually did anything, just took the money and laughed.

One day one of Elias's sergeants told him to call an inspector named Telfore, from Management Control—SFPD's version of Internal Affairs. Elias knew the call was about Sheehan. The inspector asked him to come to the Hall of Justice the next day. Inspector Telfore told him not to tell anybody. "You know how these guys get," he had said.

The next day Elias met with Telfore. He was skinny and gray. He was with another inspector whose name Elias couldn't remember. They sat him down in an interview room. It was before Elias's shift started; he was in uniform, he was sweating.

They questioned him about Sheehan. Eventually it became clear that they were only interested in a minor issue. They wanted Elias to confirm that Sheehan regularly left the district on shift. Elias, so relieved that they weren't asking about the drinking or the payoffs, told them what they wanted to know. At the end of the interview, during the handshakes goodbye, Elias—figuring that in this life you only got what you asked for—asked if they could possibly help him get transferred to a plainclothes unit. They told him they'd put in a word.

One month later Sheehan got transferred to Traffic and Elias got transferred to the Gang Task Force.

Both units were based out of Southern Station and Elias used to run into Sheehan. It was always awkward; Sheehan overcompensated, he was all handshakes and smiles. *How you doing?* he'd ask, and slap Elias on the back. *How's the big Gang Task Force?* he'd ask, his ruddy face looking truly interested.

Elias sat in his car, outside Rada Harkov's house, and wondered what ever happened to Sheehan. His mind went from Sheehan to Trammell, and he wondered what Trammell really thought about him. He liked to think he was a better partner than Sheehan had been, but he had a hard time imaging Trammell either being scared of him (like he himself had been of Sheehan) or even simply respecting him.

No other neighbors walked by. Elias didn't want to go home. He didn't want to see his wife. He wanted to walk up to Rada Harkov's door and knock and make her give him the money. He wanted to solve the case, make friends, and be happy. He wanted to save his house. He listened to sports talk on the AM radio and drank his wine.

The next day Elias and Trammell drove around the Fillmore looking for a gang member called Duda Rue. They had information that Duda Rue had shot a man named Wilkes. They drove and looked and listened to the radio.

Later their sergeant called and asked them to go with six other cops to arrest a parolee on a warrant. Elias kicked in a front door at the Banneker apartments and felt ecstatic. "You gotta kick right below the lock plate, follow through!" he yelled at Trammell afterward. He high-fived with the other cops. They looked like sports fans. The uniforms came and helped clean up and Elias and Trammell went over to Northern Station to write some quick supplemental reports about the arrest. They were back out on the street just in time to grab food.

Rada Harkov was Elias's secret, and he savored it. At lunch he didn't eat much. When their shift ended he asked Trammell to grab a beer with him. It was the last thing Trammell wanted to do, but he agreed.

They went to Ace's on Sutter Street. They had a few shots of whiskey—Elias slammed his shot glass down each time—and a few beers. Elias was quickly drunk. He sat there leaning on the bar, unconsciously mimicking Trammell's expressions. Trammell would arch one eyebrow while he listened, and so Elias would, too, which made his eyebrow quiver. Drink by drink, he was starting to talk in a different way; he was starting to talk like the bad guys did.

After the fourth shot, just when Trammell was going to make his exit, Elias opened up.

"Listen to me, man, fuck this shit, I'm gonna tell you something." His eyebrow twitched and rose. "You know that bank robbery motherfucker?"

Trammell looked at him. "Yeah."

"The one in the Richmond?"

"Yeah," repeated Trammell, looking like he was wondering where this was headed.

"I'm fin'a break that motherfucker wide open," said Elias, licking his wet lips.

"How you gonna do that?"

"Listen to me, partner," said Elias, "listen to me, buddy, I'm gonna beat that shit. On and on we—let me tell you something, you know how much money they took out of there?"

"Eight hundred racks," said Trammell.

Elias looked over his shoulder and continued in a whisper. "That's right. And guess what else? Me and you—that's our money. You hear me?" Elias raised his beer to toast, and Trammell clinked beers with him.

"You're kidding me, right?" said Trammell.

*   *   *

Later the next night Elias drove back out to Rada Harkov's street and parked and stared. The lights were on and the shades were drawn. He could solve this case. He could be on TV. He could have sex with the bank manager. He could fuck Trammell. He drank four beers and peed into an empty can. He hadn't had a panic attack all day. He wanted to sleep in the car, but it was cold and his back hurt.

Thirty minutes later he saw two cars pull up outside Rada Harkov's home. One of the cars was a black sedan and the other was a gray sports coupe. The sedan pulled into the driveway; the coupe parked in front.

Elias's left hand pulled on his seat adjuster and he let himself lean back so he was out of view. His car was about two hundred feet from the coupe, and was facing it. The coupe's lights went off, but the driver stayed put. Three men stepped out of the sedan and walked toward the front door of the house. Two of the men were younger, dressed casually in jeans and sweatshirts; the third—older, tall and bald—wore a dark suit, and seemed like the boss. The young men looked around them as they walked to the door. One of them rang the doorbell and the door swung open. Elias couldn't see if it was Rada Harkov who let them in.

Elias jotted down the coupe's license plate number. He couldn't make out the sedan's plate. He tried to take a picture with his cell phone, but it came out too dark. He was suddenly wide awake. He wished Trammell was with him. These men were gangsters, it was obvious. Elias was a member of the Gang Task Force, but he had never had any dealings with the kind of gangsters that wore suits; the gangsters he dealt with were teenagers—they killed people, but they were still teenagers.

He waited. After ten minutes the door opened again and the three men got back into their car, backed out of the driveway, and drove past him. The coupe followed behind. He ducked all the way down and then leaned back up and watched them through his rearview mirror as they turned left at the next block. He started his car and swung a quick U-turn and followed where they had turned, but the cars were already gone. He turned right, back toward where they had come from, but there was no sign of either car. He felt a mixture of anger and relief.

"Come on, Plastic Face, what I do?" Lateef Cannon yelled.

Lateef was Duda Rue's cousin. Elias was grabbing Lateef's arm and twisting it behind his back. They were on Fulton Street. It was daytime. Their feet scuffed the ground as they struggled.

"You lied, and I'm taking you in," said Elias.

"Lied on what?"

"On where your cousin is," said Elias. He twisted Lateef's arm farther. Trammell watched with his hands up like he wanted everyone to calm down.

"You smell like damn liquor, man! You drunk?" said Lateef, over his shoulder.

Trammell stepped in. "All right, come on," he said. He grabbed Elias and pulled him back. "Come on—not now," he said.

Lateef was twenty-two years old. He wore a black pea coat. He picked his black beanie off the ground and put it back on. He hadn't seen his cousin in two weeks and even if he had he wouldn't have told Elias. "Fuck you, Plastic Face! Your face all red," he said, stepping back and rubbing his arm. "I'm gonna tell my mom what you did, too."

"Fuck you," said Elias.

"You spilt my Coke," said Lateef, pointing at his drink on the ground. "I'm gonna make a complaint on your punk ass."

"Come on," said Trammell. He turned Elias and walked him back toward the car.

"You're hungover!" yelled Lateef.

Elias started to go for him again, but Trammell held him back.

They got back into the car and watched Lateef walk away. Elias, gripping the steering wheel and breathing heavy, stared at a little section of window that was fogging up.

"Fuck him," said Trammell.

After that they rode in silence for an hour until dispatch called a code 33. Someone running away from the cops over near the MLK projects. They drove fast down Webster, fast enough for Elias to forget his problems. Speeding in the car made him feel better. Maybe Elias just needed to chase more people.

Later they drove around again, looking for Duda Rue. Elias felt the need to talk about the bank growing in him. He knew that talking about it was not the right thing to do, it felt like a compulsion, but he needed to.

"Let's go out there and look around," he said. He clamped his teeth shut and looked out the window.

"Out where? The bank?" asked Trammell, seemingly able to read Elias's mind.

"Not the bank, her house."

"Whose house?"

"Rada Harkov," said Elias. He turned and looked at Trammell. Trammell stayed silent. He was hard to read.

"She's the one that did the whole thing," Elias added. He tried to will his face to relax. He could see Trammell looking right at him. He could feel a pulse in the side of his own forehead.

"She's the inside girl, the Russian. I already confirmed it with Peed."

"You asked Inspector Peed?" said Trammell. He looked shocked. His face looked transformed. He looked like he had smelled a horrible odor. "The inspector?" he asked again. It didn't make sense.

"Sam, relax, Jesus," said Elias, shaking his head and smiling a wooden smile. "I got it from a reliable source."

The light changed. Elias was suddenly sweating. His shoulders were tense and locked. He decided not to tell him about seeing the visitors stop by her house last night. Not to tell him that he had run the license plate of the gray coupe and it had come back as being registered to an eighteen-year-old girl with no criminal record.

"You doing too much."

"It's not a problem," said Elias, "I'm just working the gang thing like the sarge said. Jimmy Delarosa told me Peed was ranting and raving about how deep in it this Russian manager lady was."

"So what's that got to do with us?" asked Trammell.

"Nothing."

"So what are you going to do? You going all independent? Man, I'm supposed to be the rookie, not you."

"I'm just trying to figure it out—figure who's who and what's what, that's all."

They were interrupted again. The radio dispatch asked for a unit to respond to Page and Webster for a 211 and Elias grabbed their radio and said, "Three-adam-boy-seven, we are ten-twenty-five," and off they went, responding to a fight they had no business responding to. Elias welcomed the break from the questioning.

They were the third unit to respond. The other cops were talking to a crowd. One black woman wearing hospital scrubs was already cuffed up and sitting on the curb. The crowd was yelling at the cops.

Elias rolled the car up and asked one of the officers, "You got this?"

"Yeah, they're clear."

They rolled past the crowd and Elias asked, "Any of you seen Duda Rue?"

"Fuck you, Plastic Face, you punk-ass cracker mother-fucker," said one woman as she turned and went back to her apartment. The crowd laughed.

"Who was that?" asked Elias.

Trammell shook his head. "Nice work, Leo. You're on a roll today, baby."

Elias's head hurt. He wanted to drink. These people didn't realize that every time they said *fuck you* to him he actually

PATRICK HOFFMAN

felt it. He wanted to keep talking with Trammell, but he also wanted to shut up. He looked at Trammell. Trammell was so young. He didn't have to worry about anything. The bosses liked him. The bad guys even liked him. Life was easy for Trammell.

At 7 p.m. they stopped to eat some falafel. Elias said he had to make a call, went back out to the car, opened the trunk, and drank wine from his Gatorade bottle. He drank more than normal. He was feeling vulnerable today. He peeled an orange and pushed half of it into his mouth. The street around him seemed to be filled with twenty-year-olds. A taxi driver drove by and winked at him.

By the time he got back to the table he had regained his calm. He noted Trammell looking him over suspiciously, but he didn't care. The Arab guys were laughing quietly at the counter. He felt warmth in his stomach.

"I'm going to show you something," said Elias.

It looked like Trammell didn't want to be shown anything. He looked uneasy. He looked nervous. He knew Elias had been drinking. Elias's eyes were red and he had barely touched his food.

"I'm going to show you how to be a cop," said Elias.

"Yippee," said Trammell.

In the days that followed, Trammell would look back on that moment in the restaurant and wonder whether any other outcome had been possible. What would have happened if he had said he wasn't interested? If he had simply said no? The conversations that preceded the incident—conversations

68

that at the time he tried to tune out—played through his mind on a constant loop. He marveled at how many chances he had been given. He would tell himself it had been impossible to know what was going to happen. But then the memory of Elias's face—desperate like an addict—would pop into Trammell's mind, and Trammell would feel a blanket of guilt.

They left the falafel place and got back in the car and headed up Haight Street toward Divisadero. Elias drove to Market Street and headed toward the freeway. He radioed in that they were going to be 10-I for a while.

Elias felt nervous, but not necessarily in a bad way. He liked mischief.

"You can be a cop and do what they tell you to do," said Elias, "or you can be a cop and work for justice."

"Preach it, Reverend," said Trammell, nodding his head.

They took 101 toward the airport. Trammell asked where they were going and was told it was a surprise. Elias turned the FM radio on.

In San Bruno Elias bought a twelve-pack of Budweiser. He told Trammell to stop being so serious all the time.

They parked outside the cemetery in San Bruno and drank the beers. Trammell had never been there. He'd driven by on the way to the jail, but he'd never stopped.

"Look at all those graves," said Trammell.

Elias patronizingly told him they were soldiers. Trammell said it looked like dominoes. He kept shaking his head and looking at it.

After they drank their beers Elias drove them into the residential part of San Bruno. He parked the car a block north of Rada Harkov's house, opened the door, and said, "Come on."

Trammell got out of the car. Elias set a beer can into a blue recycling bin that was on the sidewalk. He opened the trunk, pulled out two pairs of plastic gloves and a crowbar, and then quietly pushed the trunk closed again.

"What are we doing?" asked Trammell in a whisper.

Elias smiled. "You know what we're doing."

It was true, he did know. Elias handed him a pair of the gloves.

It was dark now. Elias had never seen the house without the lights on. He didn't really have a plan. He knew he wanted to be inside. He wanted to look around. He had to do something.

Thirty feet back from the sidewalk was a gated wooden fence that led to the backyard. Elias went to the gate and tried the handle. It didn't open. He pulled a small pocket-knife from his pocket, stuck the blade through the slit in the fence near the handle, and flipped the metal latch. The door popped open, and they walked in.

Trammell closed the gate quietly behind him. They stared at each other for a moment. Then Elias tiptoed toward the house. The gravel under his feet crunched with each step. He tried the back door. It was locked. He knocked quietly on the glass, and knocked a little louder. Trammell winced. Elias pointed toward his ear, which Trammell took to mean: *listen*.

Trammell walked toward the side of the house. He slipped on his pair of gloves. They smelled like condoms. He tried a window near him; it didn't budge.

Elias was looking in through the sliding glass door. There was an informal dining room just off the kitchen. Trammell had backed away from the window and was staring at the wooden gate. "Give me that," said Elias, looking at the crowbar.

Trammell handed Elias the crowbar and looked at him like he was daring him to do it. Trammell was still only twenty-eight years old and when he was drunk, he acted younger than that. Any caution that he was feeling earlier seemed to have disappeared.

Elias took the bar and went to the window closest to the wooden gate. He put the sharp end underneath the crack of the window and inched it in. He pulled down on the bar but it slipped out from its hold. He reset the crowbar and used all his weight. The latch popped. He pushed the window open, pulled himself up, and looked in.

It was a bathroom. Elias dropped back down and motioned with two fingers pointed at his eyes and a nod of the head: *watch the gate.*

"We're just investigating, right?" whispered Trammell.

Elias nodded, pushed himself up onto the ledge of the window, thrashed his legs around, and pulled himself in with his hands, onto the sink and then the floor.

He stood up and looked around. There was a tub, some towels, and a mirror. The bathroom was tiled in large, creamy pink squares. He turned on his flashlight, then covered it with his hand. He was so nervous he could barely breathe. He felt exhilarated. The house was silent.

The hallway was dark and carpeted. He called out, "Hello, anybody home?" There was no answer.

Elias went back into the bathroom, leaned his head out, and whispered at Trammell, "I'm in." Trammell waved him off. He knew he was in.

Elias closed the window and tried to set the splintered latch back as well as he could. He walked to the back kitchen door, unlocked it, and let Trammell in.

"Go watch the front," he told Trammell.

"Did you look for an alarm?"

"Yeah, no—do it."

Trammell stepped through the kitchen. It was lit by a light above the stove. There were magazines and junk mail piled on the kitchen counter. The room smelt vaguely like garbage. Trammell looked around and walked toward the front of the house.

"Yell if you see anything," said Elias from the hallway.

"Stupid," said Trammell, walking on a light-colored carpet in the front living room. He looked behind himself as he walked to see if he was leaving tracks.

Elias walked back toward the bathroom. The house felt lived in, but not by a family. There were no toys, no signs of kids. Next to the bathroom was a bedroom. Inside the bedroom was a chest of drawers. He went to it and opened it. It was filled with neatly folded T-shirts and sweaters. He opened the five other drawers and quickly went through them. Where was the cash? There was nothing but women's clothes.

The closet was big and full. More women's clothes. Some boxes of shoes. More shoes. No men's clothes. She lived alone.

He looked under the bed and pulled out boxes from the floor. He was sweating. The boxes were filled with personal papers, letters, bills—Rada Harkov indicia.

He went to the TV stand and opened its drawers. There was nothing but movies, random wires, rubber bands, matches, and batteries.

He walked out of the bedroom and looked at a framed picture in the hallway: a crowd of adults were seated at a table, smiling up at the camera. Something about the picture—perhaps the waiter in the background wearing a tuxedo—suggested a foreign country.

"How we doing?" he called out to Trammell. There was no answer. He walked fast to the front living room and found Trammell squatting at the window. "How we doing?"

"Good, but we gotta get the fuck out of here," said Trammell, looking over his shoulder.

"Five minutes," whispered Elias.

He didn't wait for an answer. He went back into the hallway and found a door that led to the basement. He closed that door and headed for another room next to the one he had already searched. It was an office.

He grabbed a lamp and turned it on. He lowered its brightness by putting it under the desk. There was a computer on the desk and to the right of the computer a filing cabinet. He opened a file drawer and looked through it. There were financial papers, but he didn't have time for them; he wanted cash. He went to the closet and looked in. More clothes, and some white legal boxes. He pulled them down, opened them, and saw only papers inside. He tried to set them back the way he had found them. He was shaking, and a drop of sweat dripped off his head and onto the cardboard of one of the boxes. His nose was running. He breathed deep. "Okay, okay," he said out loud. He put the lamp back, turned it off, and left the room.

His flashlight made a drunken sweep of the hallway as he walked to the basement. He'd taken two steps down the stairs when he heard Trammell half whisper and half yell, "Leo!"

It sounded desperate. Elias turned on the stairs and went back up to the hallway. He tried to breathe. His mouth was as dry as sandpaper. When he reached the living room he saw the headlights of a car turn off. He heard the sound of a car door close.

Elias would later remember the next few moments so often that they seemed to become something larger than a memory. In the same way that Trammell had pinpointed exact times when he could have changed the outcome of events, Elias, for his own part, would choose this moment as the one.

"Come on!" Elias had said. Trammell was standing bent over, looking out the window.

"Come on!" Elias said again. Trammell turned his head and Elias was shocked to see him looking terrified. He looked frozen and pale. A dark figure walked past the front window. This was the moment he could have stepped forward and taken charge. They could have questioned the woman. Instead, as though Trammell's paralysis was contagious, he stood there, without moving.

Elias, his ears buzzing, heard the sound of keys jingling and nudging into the lock. He fell back a few steps toward the kitchen. The next thing he saw was Trammell standing up straight and stepping toward the door. His impression was that Trammell was going to simply open the door for the woman and they were going to have a talk.

Elias stood in the hallway and time slowed to a crawl. He held his breath. His hands were wet inside the gloves. His mouth was open; his face, set hard, had formed itself into a mask: *Plastic Face.*

He heard the door open, the sound of door on carpet. Elias felt the air leave the room. The next second he heard what sounded like a bark and then a muffled yell and two bodies falling hard on the ground. The whole house shook and echoed with the sound of a wooden boom followed immediately by the sound of glass chiming.

Elias stepped closer: Trammell was wrapped around a big ball of red hair. Their bodies were flailing. "Shut up," said Trammell, "shut up!" He looked at Elias with his hand over her mouth. "Fucking help me."

Elias backed up. *Fuck.* He could hear Trammell telling the woman to shut up again and again in a weird, high-pitched hissing voice. Elias didn't understand what was happening. Rada Harkov wasn't saying anything.

Elias, not even knowing he was doing it, hit his own head with his fist and moved toward them. He couldn't pull his gun out; it was stuck in its holster. The noise of breathing was everywhere.

Trammell struggled with her. Elias wanted to cry. He stepped toward them again. Trammell had somehow taken his own gun out and was shoving it against Harkov's neck. Legs thrashed. Elias stood above them like a referee. The situation was out of control.

Trammell was on top of her. She was facedown on the floor. They were three feet from the front door. Elias whipped his head and looked outside and saw a perfectly quiet residential street. He wanted to run.

"Okay, okay, okay, stop," said Trammell. Then to Elias, "You wanna fucking question her, question her!"

"Where's the money?" said Elias. He figured they could end this if she just answered that question. "Where's the money?" he asked again with his dry mouth.

Trammell slowly took his hand away from her face. All three of them were breathing heavily.

Trammell pushed the gun into her neck like he was going to kill her with blunt force. Elias would later remember this gesture and wonder if it marked the absolute point from which there could be no going back.

"Okay," she said quietly. Trammell pulled the gun back an inch. "Okay." They waited. "She made me do it," said Rada Harkov in her thick accent. "They said I pay. I didn't want to. They made me. It's not my idea."

"Who is she?" asked Elias.

"Sophia," she said in an exhale of breath.

Elias watched as the woman bucked up onto her hands and knees. Trammell rose up like he was riding her. Elias watched Trammell's spine go round, then flat, and he watched Rada Harkov, suddenly strong, rise up.

Trammell lifted and then drove all his weight into her and they both went toward the front door. Trammell had his left

THE WHITE VAN

forearm against the back of her neck and he landed with all of his weight on her. Elias heard the sound of her neck popping loud like a branch, and then the sound of the air leaving her lungs like a cough. Her legs went stiff and then soft. She made a clucking noise as she fought for breath. Her neck was broken. Trammell scooted back, then stood up. They watched her twitching. She twitched and gagged for an eternal moment until Trammell grabbed a pillow from the couch, turned her over by her shoulders, and put it over her head and held it down. She shook and shook and then stopped moving.

He took the pillow off her face. She lay there. The room was dark except for the orange-pink streetlights coming in through the window. Trammell stood over the body and nudged her shoulders with his hand like he was waking her from a nap. Elias realized he had his own hands on his head and he lowered them. It seemed to Elias that they were suddenly in a different room: the sofa had floral patterns, the lamp was crystal, the coffee table was glass, and there was a gas-burning fireplace.

Trammell bent down near her head and listened for breath. "She died," he whispered. He looked at Elias and asked if they should leave.

"Let's think. Let's think," said Elias. "We gotta get rid of the body. Did we leave anything? Did we bring anything in, that we need to take out?"

"The crowbar."

Elias walked over to Rada Harkov and bent down and checked for a pulse. Even with his gloves on he could feel heat coming off her neck. He closed her eyes. He could smell perfume in the air. Even in the dark, her hair was bright red. She still had keys in her hand. He wanted to throw up.

Trammell sat down on an armchair and put his face in his gloved hands. Elias stared out the front window at the street.

"Let's just burn the fucking house down," said Trammell. It sounded like he was crying.

Elias tried to list the options in his head: they could burn the house down; steal the TV and make it look like a robbery; drive her somewhere and bury her; drive her off a cliff in her own car; bury her in the backyard; put her in the car and burn the car up. Nothing felt right.

"We need to calm down and think," said Elias. "Just take a second and slow down and think."

"I'm calm," said Trammell. It was true, he did appear calm.

"What the fuck happened? Did you break her neck?"

"Yeah."

"Are you sure?"

"I felt like a little pop."

"Okay, so we got a broken neck. Now think. Grab her and let's take her to the bathroom, we'll take her and strip her and put her in the shower and make it look like she slipped on the bathtub floor. It happened once at Southern," said Elias. "Did she scratch you?"

Trammell looked over his hands and his forearms. "No."

"Did you punch her?"

"No."

"Did you bite her?"

"No."

"What'd you do when she opened the door?"

"I grabbed her and put her in a choke hold. You saw it."

Elias looked at Trammell and tried to ascertain the state of his mind. He didn't understand what happened.

"Did you bruise her neck?" Elias asked. "Did you bruise her?" he repeated, hoping in some way that by answering the question Trammell might come to realize what he'd done.

"I don't know. I don't think so."

"Fuck." Elias went and peeked out the front window. He got on his knees and looked at her. He got up and closed the blinds and turned the living room lights on, and said to Trammell that this was her routine. He turned the TV on. He examined her neck.

"I don't see anything—nothing. Come on, pick her up," said Elias. He stepped to the front door and locked the dead bolt. Trammell lifted her by the underarms and Elias took her legs. They carried her to the bathroom and set her down on her back and turned the light on. The walls were bright pink. She was lying on top of a shaggy blue bath mat. Elias's eyes went to a tangle of red hair in a trash bin.

He pulled off her coat. "Fuck me," he said as he started to unbutton her blouse. Threads popped as he pulled her shirt up over her head. He lay her body back on the floor and looked at her.

"She just attacked me," said Trammell.

Elias reached under her back and struggled with the bra. His fingers were shaking. It finally came off. He held his breath and tried not to look at her breasts.

He stood up. "Okay, take her pants off," he said to Trammell.

Trammell, businesslike, bent down and took her belt off.

"You'll have to put the belt back on them—take the pants off—leave the belt in," said Elias.

Trammell shook his head no, and set the belt on the floor. "She shit herself," he said.

Elias went to the kitchen and returned with a plastic trash bag.

"Take them off," said Elias, gesturing at her.

Trammell started to take her pants off from the top but didn't get far. He had to struggle with them, and inch them down a little at a time toward her feet before he was able to pull them all the way off.

"Why are we doing all this?" asked Trammell.

"She's taking a shower. Check her pockets," said Elias.

He did. There was nothing.

"Put the pants in here," said Elias, holding open the white trash bag. "Her underwear, too." Trammell pulled off her soiled underwear and put them in the bag. Elias tied the bag and put it on the floor.

They stepped back into the hallway. Elias looked at Trammell. His eyes were red and filled with tears. His face was slack. He was looking at his feet. He seemed younger, like a teenager. He looked up at Elias and with sudden anger said, "What the fuck you make us come here for?"

"I didn't say do that," said Elias, raising his gloved hands in a calm-down gesture.

"You saying it's my plan?" said Trammell.

"It's not your plan. Calm down."

"Fuck you."

"We're just following leads. Now, if you wanna end this thing and make a call to the San Bruno police department, call the homicide unit, fucking San Bruno whatever, I got your back one thousand percent. But if not, if you don't want to call them, then we have to think like champions. You hear me?"

Trammell nodded his head. His face looked like the face of a man who did not know how he ended up where he was.

"Okay, it's five till ten, okay? Twenty-one, fifty-five," said Elias, looking at his watch. "We gotta clean up—we gotta get that lady into the shower, we gotta fucking think about what mistakes we're making, and we gotta sneak our asses out of this place." Elias slapped Trammell on the shoulder. "Come on, snap out of it, partner."

For a moment Elias reflected on the fact that he had become the composed older partner; he had taken on the role that Sheehan played with him. He felt a small rush of pride.

He knelt down next to Rada Harkov's body. He took her right hand in his gloved hand and checked under her nails. They seemed clean. He checked her left hand. He looked at her neck for bruises and didn't see any, except for a faint blue one on the back of the neck where, presumably, she had broken it. He looked over her face. It was so strange that she could be dead. Her makeup was thick and she had blue eye shadow and red lips.

"Okay, bud, give me a hand."

They lifted her up and set her into the tub. Her body relaxed into it. They stepped back and Elias turned the water on, thought about it, and turned it back off. "We'll wait to do that," he said.

Elias looked around the bathroom. "You come home and take a shower, what do you do?" He seemed to be talking to Rada Harkov.

He walked out of the bathroom and Trammell followed. "You walk into the house"—he sounded like a lawyer making closing arguments—"you walk in and take your coat off. Grab her coat from the hallway," he directed Trammell, pointing toward the coat.

Trammell left and came back and handed it to him. Elias checked her pockets and put the coat on an armchair. He bent down and cleaned up her purse, which had fallen on the ground. Inside the purse was her cell phone. Trammell watched as Elias pressed buttons and breathed through his nose and looked at the call history list. "Grab some paper from her office," the older man said. Trammell returned with the paper.

Elias instructed Trammell to write down the names and numbers as he read them off. He was looking for Russian-sounding names; he found someone named Dmitri Komar. He spelled the name and gave Trammell a number in the 415 area code. He found a Gregory, a Hilda, a Lexi, and then in S's, he found what he was looking for. "Sophia—bingo, that's our girl, that's where the money's at. Sophia, 415-610-1649. You got it?"

"Got it."

Elias looked through the rest of her call history and didn't see anything noteworthy.

He turned toward Trammell and started up again. "She comes in, she leaves her coat, she puts her phone right here."

He put the phone down on the coffee table. "She turns on the TV—already did that. She walks into the kitchen." They walked into the kitchen. "She goes to the refrigerator, she opens it. She grabs a bottle of chardonnay, pours a glass." Elias pulled the cork from a half-full bottle, poured some into a glass, and set it on the table. Then he poured the wine from the glass into the sink and looked at Trammell, who seemed to be in a trance. Elias walked to the bathroom and touched the empty glass to Rada Harkov's right hand, then, to her red lips. He raised the glass and looked at the little red mark of lipstick and wondered whether the crescent was upside down or not—it didn't really matter, lipstick was lipstick. He looked at himself in the mirror and returned to the kitchen. He filled the glass halfway up again and set it back down on the counter. "She drinks wine," he said. He raised the bottle, and without touching his lips to it, he poured some wine into his mouth.

"Okay," he continued, "I take some leftovers and I set them here next to the wine, but first I want to take a little shower, so . . ."

They went to the bedroom. Elias threw her shirt and bra into the hamper. "Drawer," he said, pointing at the drawer. "Grab some clean underwear, can't have her be all . . . you know, in the hamper," he finished, pointing at it. Trammell went to the chest of drawers and opened up the topmost compartment and looked at the underwear. He hated Elias. He didn't understand this. He felt so tired. He looked at Elias and considered strangling him, but instead picked up a new pair of underwear and placed them on the hamper.

Elias lifted a white bathrobe off a hook on the door and stepped out of the room.

They walked back to the bathroom and Elias hung the bathrobe in its place. "There," he said. Elias took a deep breath. Despite everything, he was enjoying himself. He couldn't help it. He was scared, he felt sick, he was mad, but he also hadn't felt so good in a long time. He felt euphoric. *I'm the composed one*, he thought. He breathed in and looked around. His eyes settled on the window he had come in through. With the light on he could see how the wood had splintered where the latch had given way. He stepped to it and again set the latch back as well as he could. He then grabbed a tube of toothpaste from the sink and squeezed some white paste onto his gloved finger and smoothed it into the splintered part of the sill. He added some more. It looked, at least to the glancing eye, as though it had never been damaged.

Elias stepped back and examined his work. He turned and looked at Trammell and raised his eyebrows, as though he were saying, "Not bad, right?" Trammell answered by looking away.

Elias then turned his attention to Rada Harkov's body. He stared at her. "We gotta deal with her makeup," he said. The showerhead was detachable and he took it off and turned the water on and aimed a weak stream at her face. "Grab me a pot from the kitchen—keep your gloves on—a spaghetti pot." Trammell turned and walked to the kitchen.

When he came back Elias took the pot from him and set it under the spigot in the tub and filled it with warm water. He lifted the pot and poured half of it over the dead woman's head. He grabbed a wooden bath brush and scrubbed her face with it. Poured water on her head again and filled the pot and poured it once more, and then began to scrub her face almost violently.

"Don't fuck her up," said Trammell. His rage was growing.

Elias took some shampoo from the edge of the tub and lathered up her red hair. "She was washing her hair when she slipped and fell." He dabbed little clouds of shampoo on her hands. "There," he said.

He set the showerhead right and turned it on. A stream of water fell down onto Rada Harkov's body.

"Fucking SOB of a night," said Elias.

3

Two weeks before the bank robbery, the man who had met Emily in the bar, the man who had taken her to the hotel, drugged her, and driven her to the bank, "the Russian" (his real name was Benya Stavitsky), had received his final warning on missed payments from another Russian, a money-lender named Yakov Radionovich. Benya had fallen behind on a loan that originated sixteen months earlier on friendly terms at $15,000 and had grown in further loans, interest, and theft to reach the unfriendly level of $120,000.

Benya was forty-five years old. He was from Moscow. He bought and sold Chinese merchandise at the Alameda Port. He would take these goods and sell them at a small profit to vendors in different Chinese suburbs—Fremont, Antioch, Richmond, San Jose. If a shipment of Chinese soccer balls ended up sitting at the port, he was one of the people who (through a third party) would bid on it. He fancied himself a businessman, but essentially he was a black market trader.

The original loan of $15,000 had been taken out in order to buy a thousand cartons of Zhong Nan Hai, Red Sun

Edition cigarettes, at a cost of $12,000. The extra three thousand was for rent and car payments. He'd planned on selling the cigarettes for $20,000. Benya had known Yakov Radionovich socially around San Francisco, and had heard people say that Radionovich loaned money. He was also familiar with rumors suggesting that Radionovich was a gangster.

Radionovich was an ugly man: his face sagged, it was peppered with moles, he was bald, skinny, and tall. His appearance made him seem more bureaucratic than criminal, but whenever Benya had encountered him at weddings or family celebrations, he had always acted rather nicely. The Russian community in San Francisco was large in number, but small in how one would always seem to run into the same people.

It was at one of these family gatherings that Benya Stavitsky worked up the courage to ask Radionovich if they could speak about "a small piece of business." Radionovich touched Benya lightly on the arm and looked at him as if he had just received both good and bad news; his eyes went over Benya's face like a man reading print. He then he pulled out a business card from his jacket pocket and told Benya to call on Monday morning.

After that first exchange Benya had walked toward the bar feeling especially uplifted, thinking in Russian: *That was easy.* He also felt like people at the party were watching him admiringly, as though they recognized two important men discussing important business.

They met the following Monday at Nefedovna's Tea Room on Balboa Avenue. Radionovich must have been family with the owners; the restaurant was closed, but the doors had been left unlocked, and Radionovich—smoking a cigarette and talking on a cell phone—was waiting outside.

Benya arrived at the meeting nervous. Earlier, he had stood alone in his living room and practiced his presentation, practiced the way he was going to carry himself during the meeting, how he was going to ask for the loan. This proved unnecessary. After making many inquiries into the health of this acquaintance or that, Radionovich had simply asked how much money Benya wanted. Benya answered by saying, $15,000.

The deal was swift and informal. Radionovich gave Benya a piece of paper with the address of an office in Daly City and told him to come there the next day.

And so, the next day, an uncharacteristically hot one, Benya went to the office on Hillside Boulevard, in Daly City. It was a gray building in the midst of other gray buildings. There was an American name on the door, O'Brien & Associates. The name was printed on the glass, and behind the glass was a dusty plastic door shade. Not knowing whether to knock or just enter, Benya opted for the latter.

An electric bell rang somewhere. There was no receptionist working. Radionovich came from the back, smiling with his hand stretched out, ready to shake. Benya began to take his jacket off, but Radionovich told him not to bother.

After exchanging pleasantries, before they could even sit down, the $15,000 was given to Benya in the form of fifteen money orders, each one written for $1,000. There was only the amount written on it, no payee, and Radionovich made sure to point this out, telling Benya not to lose it, because "any soul" could pick it up and cash it if he did. Benya felt a tinge of trepidation as the money was handed over, but he dismissed it as irrational, and put the money orders into the breast pocket of his coat. He asked about interest and Radionovich winced. "No interest for the first two months, after that twenty to thirty-three percent of the loan, per month—typical," he said with a shrug. Benya suppressed a smile. *Two months?* He offered to write up a receipt, but Radionovich waved the idea off.

The "opportunity" Benya had taken the loan for, the deal for the Red Sun cigarettes, had been brought to him by a man named Huang Pei Tian. Benya had had previous dealings with Mr. Huang, albeit much smaller ones, and he felt he could trust him.

Mr. Huang was in his early thirties. He was balding, and he usually wore clothes that suggested an active nightlife, a thick gold chain, or a fancy watch. He lived in Oakland's Chinatown, and Benya had been inside his crowded house before to pay for merchandise. He had bought goods from Mr. Huang on half a dozen occasions. The profits were derived from a simple evasion of U.S. taxes and discounted prices for lost or stolen products.

Mr. Huang had called and explained the terms of the deal to Benya in a giddy English a week earlier. He'd said it was a "once-in-a-year deal, man, top-line China smokes, can't beat it."

As soon as Benya had the money, he called Mr. Huang and told him he could come right over. When he got to the house in Oakland, Mr. Huang, who had been waiting outside his front door, jumped in Benya's car and shook his hand in a way that suggested regret.

"Man, you went too slow," said Mr. Huang with a smile. "They left—sold those cigarettes cheap and took off."

Benya couldn't believe his ears. Why had he driven over here? Why had he borrowed the money? "You could have told me," he said, trying to be amicable.

"Man, they move too fast. That deal was so good, it just sold up," said Mr. Huang. "They coming back in two weeks, though."

"Who are they?" asked Benya.

"They Chinese from Taiwan, they got a good line, man, really nice."

"Then you call me when they come back," said Benya, attempting to sound professional. Depression had descended.

Two days later he got the call. They were back. But they could only do it for a bigger shipment. Forty thousand dollars for five thousand cartons. "Fucking Camels, no Red Sun shit, man, real Camels," said Mr. Huang. "That's seventy-five thousand dollars' worth, easy. I can put ten thousand dollars down, for a quarter." His voice muffled through the phone with excitement.

Benya called Yakov Radionovich and set up a meeting. He explained the situation and asked for another loan. Radionovich asked all the relevant questions and eventually agreed to Benya's request. He'd give him another $15,000, but he explained that he would need to be paid back within two months or Benya would be charged an additional "fee" of $10,000, bringing the total to $40,000. Benya agreed. Yakov Radionovich hinted that Benya would not have problems moving the cigarettes.

After that Benya asked if Radionovich could possibly provide a few men for protection. He didn't want to seem unsavvy, but he was used to dealing in thousands, not tens of thousands of dollars. Radionovich agreed to provide two men for backup.

For the next day or two Benya went back and forth with Mr. Huang about how the money would be exchanged, how the cigarettes would be examined and tested, who would be allowed to come, and where the deal would happen; Mr. Huang's tone during all of these calls suggested that Benya's questions were those of a neophyte. It was finally agreed that they would do it right at the port in Oakland, berth 21-70, at nine o'clock the following Sunday morning.

On Sunday, Benya—carrying $30,000 hidden in the trunk of his car—picked up Yakov Radionovich's two men (they were young and quiet), drove to Oakland, picked up Mr. Huang, and was directed to the Port of Oakland. A driver with a truck was waiting for Benya's call on Dolphin Street, near the port.

At the gate Mr. Huang popped out of the car and talked to the guard sitting inside the booth. They then drove to the far side of the port and pulled up to a trailer, where they were waved into a parking spot. Before they could even open the doors, two Chinese men were bearing down on them with AK-47s. Benya was naive; at first he thought this must be part of the procedure. It became clear that it wasn't when the two men were joined by five others and Mr. Huang was pulled from the car and beaten with a baseball bat. The two

Russians never even had a chance to pull out their guns (if, in fact, they even had them).

Benya and the Russians were ordered down on the ground. It took about twenty seconds for the Chinese men to find the money. They were gone ten seconds after that.

The next day Benya went to visit Mr. Huang in the hospital. He had checked out. Benya found him at home. Mr. Huang, bandaged and limping, did not invite Benya in; he spoke to him through the doorway and said there was nothing he could do. He had lost $10,000 of his own money, he reminded Benya. Benya insisted Mr. Huang tell him who the Chinese men were; surely Yakov Radionovich could help him get the money back.

"They're Zhu Lien Bang," Mr. Huang said. "United Bamboo. We're fucked, man."

When Benya went to Radionovich he was told there was nothing he could do except offer another loan. "Live in the black market, die in the black market," Radionovich said in Russian.

The loans went up: fifty thousand, sixty thousand, eighty thousand. Benya Stavitsky was ruined.

At the time of the initial loan, Benya lived by himself in a clean two-bedroom apartment near the end of Cabrillo Avenue, deep in the Richmond District. By the time the loan had grown to $120,000, he had moved to a new apartment. His car had been repossessed, and he was surviving on a diet of potatoes, pasta, bread, tea, and cigarettes.

The new apartment was in the nice part of the Tenderloin—near Nob Hill—and while his building didn't have a name, it was within sight of buildings like the Steinhart, the Mithila, the Granada, and the Hotel Carlton. The exterior of the building looked like it had been stained by tobacco smoke.

Benya had enough sense and common decency to let Radionovich know he had changed addresses. He had handwritten a note on stationery, saying he was moving and that he had every intention of repaying the debt. He included his new address (1007 Sutter Street, apartment 717) and a few words expressing how kind Radionovich had been.

The truth was Benya was angry at Radionovich. He couldn't help thinking Radionovich knew the Chinese men. He must have known them. The world was small.

One day Benya Stavitsky was lying fully dressed on his bed in his new studio apartment, trying to come up with ways of making money and dreaming about being a boy in Moscow. There was a knock on the door. He figured it must be his neighbor who was always asking for cigarettes.

He was surprised and embarrassed to see Radionovich—dressed up as usual in a coat and tie—standing at the threshold with a very sad look on his face. Benya stood frozen with the door open, embarrassed mainly over the state of his current living situation. In his mind he was at least an equal to Radionovich in terms of being a businessman; and yet, here he was, standing in his small studio apartment with no prospects. It was clear, they were not equals.

They spoke in Russian. "Yakov Radionovich, I am so happy to see you," Benya said.

"Thank you, my friend," said Radionovich, leaning in a bit to look into the room. "I was in the neighborhood."

"Of course, please come in," said Benya, opening the door and stepping back to make room.

The apartment was tiny, but neat: the bed was made; a few books (business books and a self-help book, all in English and all from the library) were stacked on a nightstand. There was a metal kitchen table with Benya's keys on it a few feet from the bed; the kitchen was just beyond the table.

Radionovich walked into the room and sniffed around as though he was searching for a foreign scent. He slipped his shoes off.

"Would you like some tea?"

"No, thank you. I'm only here for a minute."

Benya pulled out one of the two folding chairs from the table and awkwardly set it down near the window. He did not know what he was doing. "Please, sit," he said.

Radionovich took off his coat, folded it, sat down, and set the coat on his lap. The man looked very tired. He stared at Benya, searching for words.

"The debt," Radionovich finally said, shaking his head, "is out of my hands."

Benya didn't understand what the words meant, but he understood the tone. He felt nauseous.

"I have done all that I could," continued Radionovich. "I have given you chance after chance. But I have my own concerns and my own problems, and I have been forced to trade your debt to someone else."

For a brief moment Benya felt relieved. This was the bad news that necessitated such formality?

"I am sorry," continued Radionovich, and then, in English: "It is out of my hands."

"So who—surely I can make arrangements with . . ." said Benya in Russian. He couldn't finish his thought.

"I understand. I came to tell you. You are my friend. They will come and explain things. But please, Benya, please, listen to me, please do not disappoint them. I am nice. These things happen. Unfortunately, they may not see things the same as you and I."

Benya felt a wave of dread and anger rising in him. His face was hot and he was ashamed to think he may have been blushing. His forehead was damp. The world seemed organized against him. Radionovich sat and stared.

"Are they Russian?" asked Benya. Maybe he knew them. Maybe they would agree to extend the loan, or even loan him a little bit more to get him out of this damned hole he was in. If he just had time.

"They will speak to you," answered Radionovich. "They will speak to you." He nodded his head, signifying that the conversation was over. Benya didn't want to acknowledge this; he sat there blank-faced and stared at Radionovich's lap. After a few seconds Radionovich rose to leave. He put his shoes back on, balancing his ankle on his shin. At the door he turned back to Benya, shook his hand like an American, gave a final shrug, and left the apartment.

Benya grabbed for his cigarettes on the table and knocked a spoon to the floor; the superstition that a woman would be visiting passed through his mind, and he dismissed it as absurd. He stood by the window and smoked and looked down on Sutter Street and contemplated what Radionovich had said. Surely they would be open to extending the loan. Why didn't he ask that? What was this business about trading the debt? He only owed Radionovich $80,000 in actual cash if you got rid of the "interest." Radionovich must have sold the debt for between $80,000 and $100,000. Would it really be worth it to pick up the debt for a profit of $20,000? What kind of person trades a debt? Benya decided he would go at them hard and firm and demand he only pay on the actual loan and not the so-called interest. You can't charge "interest" on a loan that was never written down in the first place.

He thought about leaving San Francisco. He had been here for six years. He had no real connections. He could go anywhere, Brooklyn, Florida, Tel Aviv, Paris. Surely these debt collectors wouldn't follow him wherever he went. He was forty-five years old; he could start over. He flicked his cigarette out the window and watched it spin down to the sidewalk. No, he wouldn't run, he was a businessman, he could make the money back. He had run from Russia and things had only gotten worse. He would meet with this new man and together they would come up with a plan.

Three days later, at seven o'clock on a Wednesday morning, Benya heard three knocks on his door and knew instantly that they had come. He was already dressed and drinking tea and looking at Facebook when they knocked. He closed his computer and stared at the door wondering if there was any way to avoid what was waiting out there.

Without asking who it was, he unchained, unbolted, and opened the door. He was surprised to see a motherly-looking woman. She appeared to be in her fifties, or sixties. She wore a plain, woman's pantsuit. Benya felt a moment of relief— it must be the wrong door. But no, she lifted a hand that was holding a card and said in an accented Russian, "Good morning, my dear. My name is Sophia Kamenka and I am the holder of your debt." Benya glanced at the card. He didn't know what to say.

"May we come in?" she asked.

Benya opened the door wider and saw a man standing behind her. The man was looking at his own shoes as if he was shy. He appeared to be in his mid-thirties. He had a military-style haircut, he wore combat boots, jeans, and a black bomber jacket. He didn't look particularly frightening, but he seemed ugly—his brows were swollen, and he had blue and bugged eyes. Benya measured the man's shoulders and looked at his jaw and his skin and decided that even if he wasn't large there was something a bit menacing about him. Benya opened the door and let them pass.

"So . . . I," began Benya in Russian. "Would you like some tea?"

"No, thank you," said Sophia. She walked through the small apartment, looking at everything. The man with her stood by the door and watched Benya.

"You are Ukrainian?" asked Benya, hearing her accent. She looked Jewish.

"My family was from Odessa," said Sophia. "But I lived all over the Black Sea." She continued: "And I lived in Moscow for a few years."

She walked over to Benya, stood within a foot of him, stared up into his face with a questioning look, and said, "You owe us quite a large sum of money."

"And I will pay it back in full, all eighty thousand dollars. I just need six months to put a few ideas into motion," he said to her.

She smiled and took his hand in her own. "It's not eighty thousand, Benya Stavitsky, and you know it; you know perfectly well it's more than that."

He decided not to argue and stayed silent.

She ticked her head to the side and the young man at the door came into the room and walked to Benya's computer. Benya tried to step toward the man, but the woman positioned herself between them. The man opened the computer and stared at Benya's Facebook page. He clicked on Benya's friends' icon and scrolled through the list of friends, staring as though he were memorizing them. He then pulled the plug from the wall, closed the computer, and set the power cord on top of it.

The man moved to Benya's writing desk and pulled open the drawers. Benya again tried to step to the man, but Sophia again blocked his way. The man took out papers and looked at them. There wasn't much there. He took his time with each document. The papers he wasn't interested in were dropped to the ground; the good ones were set on the desk. He found Benya's old maroon Russian passport, opened it, looked through every page, and then put it into his own back pocket.

Benya could not believe what was happening. It was rude. He could not have dreamed up a scenario where this type of behavior would be considered acceptable. His blood pressure rose. He was a man of principles and manners and this young man was looking through his personal belongings. It was like he was back in Moscow: the mafia was everywhere. He wanted to say something, but he couldn't. Sophia continued to hold his hand. He tried to pull it back, but she only tightened her grip and smiled up at him. The room spun. The sound of honking came incessantly from the street below.

"It's fine," she said in English, reaching up and touching his shoulder with her free hand.

The young man went to Benya's bed and pulled the mattress off the frame and the sheets off the mattress and examined the seams on all sides. He felt the mattress methodically. He spent a good few minutes doing this.

"What do you want?" Benya finally managed to say.

"We just want to look around. We want to meet our new client," said Sophia, finally releasing his hand. "Intake interview," she said, switching to English and stressing the sound of the *t*'s.

Benya had to sit down. He put his hands in his pockets.

The young man set the mattress to the side and began examining the metal bed frame. He looked inside the nightstand next to the bed. He leafed through the pages of Benya's books and even seemed to read the back of one of them. He lifted the nightstand up and examined the bottom and then the inside of it, running his fingers along the edges. He set it right again and put the books back on it.

"You are good with people?" asked Sophia, waking Benya from a trance.

"I don't know," said Benya.

"You are. I know. I see you and I know. People persons are handsome or gentle, you know what I mean; you are both. In Russia you were a . . . ?"

"I studied engineering," said Benya (he was a liar).

"And here you are a . . . ?"

"I am a businessman."

"A salesman?"

"A trader," said Benya, looking down at his feet.

The woman smiled ambiguously and looked around the room.

The young man had been walking a small circle, studying the walls. Benya could not imagine what he was looking for, so he sat there and smoked; he had shown them his pack of cigarettes before he lit one, asking for permission: *dog!* The young man went to an air shaft near the kitchen, moved a chair, took out a Leatherman from his pocket, unscrewed the grill, removed it, and looked inside with a small flashlight.

Sophia sat down across from Benya and stared at him with her head cocked slightly to the side, like she was appreciating a piece of art. The tip of her tongue showed on her lip.

The young man walked over to the closet and looked through all of Benya's clothes, checking every pocket, even appearing to look at the labels and sizes of things.

Benya looked at Sophia. She was making a sympathetic face, like she too was mystified by what was happening.

The young man studied all six of Benya's pairs of shoes, tossing them with thuds onto the floor as he went. Next he found two large cardboard legal boxes at the back of the closet and carried them to the table. He set them down in front of Sophia, who began to look through them.

Benya was fuming. "Perhaps I can help you?" he said, his voice shaking.

"Shhh . . ." said Sophia, not even looking up from the papers.

The young man disappeared into Benya's bathroom. He came back out and went to the kitchen, where he noisily began taking out all of the pots and pans and dishes and looking into the cabinets with his flashlight. The noise he was making now seemed intentional; dishes and silverware clanged on the floor.

"Give me your wallet," said Sophia, standing and holding her hand out.

"Why?"

"Give me your wallet," she repeated in English.

"Look," said Benya, standing and backing toward the door. "I owe you the money, I will pay you the money, but this—this is unacceptable. I have not even met you yet."

The room fell silent.

Sophia moved her hand and the young man stepped toward Benya, who stepped back against the wall. Benya raised his hands in surrender. The young man gave a tiny smile and then faked at Benya's face. Benya hadn't fought since he was a boy in Moscow. He flinched up hard and the young man came back with his left hand and punched him square in the balls. Benya fell to the ground, and unable to breathe or yell, curled into the fetal position.

The young man produced an extendable baton from somewhere and whipped it open. Benya heard it snap and clenched his body and covered as the thing was raised up.

"No," said Sophia. "Please."

The young man stepped back.

"Give me the wallet," said Sophia.

Benya could not straighten up, even to grab his wallet. He felt sick, his head hurt, his stomach hurt, he could not breathe, *fucking Radionovich*.

The young man stepped into the kitchen, filled a glass with water, and drank it. Except for Benya's breathing, they were all silent.

After half a minute, Benya pushed himself up onto his knees. He tried to grab his wallet, but he couldn't. He got all the way up and nearly fainted. He pulled out his wallet and limped to the table and set it down.

Benya could smell the leather of the wallet. Sophia looked through it. She took out the different business cards of his associates and examined each one. She took out his credit cards, looked them over, and put them back. She took out his driver's license and handed it to the young man, who put it with the passport in his back pocket. She pulled out his cash and counted forty-two dollars; she arranged the bills faceup and then snapped her fingers and the young man handed her five one-hundred-dollar bills, which she added to Benya's cash before depositing it all back into his wallet. "It's not a great quality wallet," she said in English, setting it down on the table.

She stood up and put Benya's laptop and power cord into one of the legal boxes and put his cell phone from the table on top of that and said, "Listen to me, my dear, you owe us one hundred and sixty thousand dollars. This is a remarkable sum of money. You know, I know, we all know that people get killed for much less. People like say, for instance, your aunt Galina in Petrovka? Or your friend David in Miami? Your ex-wife, the American, in Fresno?" She looked to the young man, who nodded. Benya's mind reeled; how did she know about his aunt Galina? She wasn't even on Facebook. Sophia continued, "Maybe she can pay, this ex-wife? I don't know. I do know this makes me sick to think about it in these terms—but this is where we find ourselves. I have given you a gift of five hundred dollars to hold you over for the next few days. Consider it a signing bonus. You're not alone. It's a little problem. Just wait here for the time being. We will tell you when we are ready. But please, please, dear heart, do not worry about a single little thing."

She pointed at the boxes and Benya watched as the young man stacked the two of them up with the computer at the top and walked out the door with it all in his arms.

Sophia looked at Benya for a short moment and then turned and left, closing the door gently behind her as she went.

Benya spent the next three days close to home. If he went out it was only to buy cigarettes or wine. He didn't spend any of the five hundred dollars, but the bills, crisp and new, were there each time he took out his wallet.

He was feeling guilty. He had a core of guilt in his chest and it was growing by the day. It felt like an actual physical presence in there, like if he reached into his insides he would be able to grab on to a black, wet tumor of guilt. Guilt and shame.

What did Sophia mean when she said, *We will tell you when we are ready*? What were they looking for in his room?

Why did they take his papers and his passport? Should he call his family and warn them about this woman?

He attempted to call Yakov Radionovich at least ten times from a pay phone in a Laundromat on Hyde Street. Each time it would go to an answering machine, and each time Benya would not leave a message. What could he say?

He played with the idea of going to the police, but because of the threats to his family he decided he couldn't. He didn't trust the police. American police were unintelligible. He felt friendless. The few friends he had wouldn't understand. He would have to go over all the embarrassing details.

This wasn't the first time he had experienced something like this. In Russia, after the collapse, he had helped open a clothing store in Moscow. It hadn't been a big shop; he and his older cousin Dmitri ran it together, selling knock-off sporting clothes. The shop was in the Strogino district, one stop away from their apartment. They had hired their neighborhood *krysha* to protect them and things had gone fine for a month, until one evening before they closed, three men came in, closed the front door, and locked it. The men were giants. They each weighed over 250 pounds. They wore the warm-up suits and the kind of gold chains that were fashionable for thugs during that time. The largest of the three men, mustached and oily, walked up to Dmitri and introduced himself in a friendly way. The man explained that times were dangerous and that every small business on Ulitsa Kulkova Street needed to pay for protection. Dmitri told the man that he already was paying, that Ilya from the Towers was their *krysha*. The man smiled at Dmitri, looked around the store, and asked where Ilya was. He asked if he could please speak to Ilya. The other two men laughed. The man then told Dmitri that their terms of protection equaled 10,000 rubles a month. Dmitri was already paying Ilya 3,000 rubles a month, and that was eating into their profits. Dmitri told the man it was bullshit, and that if he wanted money he would have to go to Ilya. The men left the store, saying they would come back for payment in one week, and if Ilya from the Towers had anything to say about it he should be there, too.

Dmitri and Benya had gone to Ilya and told him about the men. They described the men and Ilya had seemed to think it was funny. Ilya told Dmitri that the bigger man was his cousin; that he was a police officer, and that the type of protection he was selling was different than Ilya's; it was state protection.

Dmitri stopped paying Ilya. He refused to pay the new men. On the two-month anniversary, right after they opened the shop, the new men came back in. Dmitri told Benya to run out the back and get the police. Benya ran to the police. He tried to get them to come back to the store with him, but the officer, a kid who looked like he couldn't grow a beard, had told him that he was not allowed to leave his post. The officer told Benya he would call it in, and Benya watched as he turned away and spoke into his walkie-talkie.

Benya ran back to the store. He came in from the back and found Dmitri on the ground with his head smashed in. Benya drove Dmitri to the hospital, where he died three days later. Benya left Russia the next week, first for Finland, then Paris, New York, and finally, San Francisco.

* * *

On the third day after he was visited by Sophia he decided he couldn't wait around his apartment any longer. He went to the main library and sat on a bench and watched homeless people. The Tenderloin was filled with addicts—people with their faces deformed by drugs, asking him if he was all right. *Look at this place. Look at that woman, she doesn't have a chin.*

That night, after hours of tossing and turning in his bed, he dreamed of a six-headed snake: all of the heads extended out from the center, like a wheel, six tongues hissing and the thing's skin oily and green. He woke up covered in sweat and began his fourth day of waiting before the sun arose.

Eighteen hours later, for the first time in his life, he found himself smoking crack in a hotel with Emily. Sophia and the man had come for him earlier that morning and searched the Tenderloin for, as Sophia phrased it, "the right girl." They had driven in circles for what felt like hours until they had settled on Emily. Nobody had told him anything. He didn't know what they were doing; he had no idea what the plan was. He sat silently in the back of the white van until they told him he had to meet *that girl.* They followed Emily as she walked around the Tenderloin. They watched her talk to some teenage Asians on Leavenworth and they followed her to a bar. "Show her these drugs and make her come back to the hotel, room 214," Sophia said, handing him a card for a hotel in South San Francisco, a key with number 214 printed on it, and a bag filled with drugs. "Show her money, show her drugs; get her to go with you."

Benya protested that he couldn't, that he didn't know how to do these kinds of things.

"Use your fucking face," Sophia said in English, "and know her. Get to know her." He didn't know what this meant, and he felt fear in his belly. "Show her the drugs," Sophia repeated. "She will go with you." They told him they would be in the hotel room directly next to his.

And now he was so high, his eardrums were buzzing. He had never used any kind of drug before. He paused on the balcony outside and looked out at the courtyard of the hotel. There were trees he hadn't noticed; their leaves shook with the wind. Everything was focused; he was focused. The walkway was vivid. Things were strangely good. He knocked softly on the next door, room 216. Sophia opened it and stepped aside, frowning at his obvious intoxication. He smelled like chemicals.

"What you are going to do with her?" he said in Russian. He didn't feel scared, he felt collegial. He felt in control.

"I told you, nothing—tonight, nothing. I promise you, on my mother's name, we are not going to harm this girl. It is just a little scam we will do—*using* her, mind you. Not *on* her. She is a partner, like you and me and him." She pointed at the ugly man who was sitting there looking tired.

The sound of the television playing next door was coming in through a laptop in their room; they were listening to everything. There was a video feed, too; he walked over to it and watched Emily sitting on a chair, holding the pipe, looking around the room.

"I don't know if I can do this," said Benya. The drugs were making him bold enough to voice his concern.

"You don't have a choice." said Sophia. She walked over to the bathroom and rummaged through a bag until she found a small glass vial. She shook it and held it out for him. "Put this in her drink."

"What is it?"

"It won't hurt her." She handed him the vial, and then pulled out ten twenty-dollar bills. "And this, to pay for her time. See, she's happy, we're happy, you're happy."

"What am I going to tell her?"

"Tell her what I've told you." Sophia was starting to sound angry. She looked to the young man for assistance, but he merely shrugged. "Tell her we plan on making *money*," she said. "Tell her, you know, I'm your wife and we are running a little scheme; tell her we will fill her in when the time comes. Use your imagination. No more baby talk. If she wants to leave, she can leave. She will not be at risk—but if she does leave—you"—she pointed her finger at Benya—"*you* will be at risk."

Benya held the vial in his hand and looked at it. What was he becoming? He turned to leave. The young man rattled a bottle of pills, and when Benya looked, tossed them over to him.

"And give her those," said Sophia. "Her medicine. She'll be happy."

The next six days were strange ones for Benya Stavitsky. They were the strangest days of his life, but they were also very boring. He sat around. Sometimes he watched the girl, sometimes Sophia did, sometimes they both did. The young man ("Georgy," Sophia called him) barely went into Emily's room. He just watched Emily via the computer, or lay on one of the beds, or watched television. He never left the hotel.

Benya tried to suss out what the relationship between Sophia and the young man, Georgy, was. They certainly didn't seem to communicate very much. There was no bantering. Benya started to wonder if he could gain any traction with Georgy, but anytime he tried to talk with him (when Sophia was out of the room), he was rebuffed. He didn't push the issue—he didn't want to risk another beating, or worse.

Benya observed Sophia reporting information about how the girl was doing to Georgy, who would sit there and nod passively. Occasionally, when Benya was in Emily's room, he would try to listen for sounds coming through the wall; a difficult task, since he knew they might be watching him on their computer. He would take up a relaxed pose and strain his ears as hard as he could. On two occasions he thought he heard Sophia and Georgy arguing.

Benya had no idea what they planned on doing with Emily. At first, he figured it must be some kind of sexual thing, some kind of prostitution, or pornography, but then it seemed that Sophia was grooming Emily for some type of bank fraud. Benya would listen to her telling Emily that she was just going to make a little transaction. It seemed too easy to be true. It had to be worse.

And why did they keep drugging her? They were giving Emily different drugs, a liquid in her drink, the pills, the crack, and at night, most disturbingly, Sophia would pull back Emily's blanket, pull down her pants, and inject shots from a small syringe to the inside of her thigh. Even this would not wake Emily. But to what end were they drugging her? Benya didn't know, but he could see that Georgy, who only came in the room when Emily was unconscious, took a keen interest in these daily administrations.

And they tested Emily. By the third day, Sophia was making her do strange little tasks. Emily was asked to walk here or there, to write down things, to clean things, to step outside and come back in, to memorize information. Benya tried to recognize a pattern, but he couldn't.

The thought of escape was always on his mind. He thought of running nearly every hour. He wanted no part of what they were doing. But the obverse of this sentiment was the prospect of clearing his debt—*to start fresh!* And there was still the matter of the threats they had made in his apartment—credible threats—to his aunt, his ex-wife, and his friend. They had access to his Facebook account by now, and if they wanted, they could reach out and kill acquaintances barely even known to Benya. The fact of the matter was, leaving felt scarier than staying. His stomach was a knot of fear. What would they do to Emily if he left? He told himself he was staying to make sure nothing bad— nothing "untoward," as Sophia innocuously put it—would happen to her. But in the end, it wasn't altruism that was keeping him there; it was fear.

After the first night, Benya would occasionally smoke crack with Emily. He did it because it seemed to lessen his fear. Sophia and the young man never objected—in fact, they seemed to encourage it. It wasn't like he was getting out of control; he would just occasionally smoke from the pipe. It helped quiet his mind. They were giving him a constant supply to give to her, and he shared it.

It didn't help him sleep. He would spend the night in the room with Sophia and the young man. They would take shifts watching Emily, either in her room or on the computer. Benya slept on the carpeted floor in their room. He had a blanket and a pillow that he had stolen from Emily's room on the third night. Georgy also slept on the floor (he snored gutturally); Sophia slept—fully dressed and over the covers—on the only bed in the room. When it was Benya's turn to watch Emily, one of them would shake him awake and he would go into her room and sit on the reading chair and wait. If she stirred (she rarely did), he was supposed to wake the others up.

Meanwhile, Benya, Sophia, and Georgy did the regular things that people do. They never seemed regular, though. When Benya brushed his teeth, he felt self-conscious. When he used the bathroom, he felt self-conscious (*the noises!*). When he ate food—always delivery—he felt strange and unhappy. Sophia ordered the food unenthusiastically. Georgy smacked his lips, ate with his head down, and swallowed loudly. Their trash overflowed from the bathroom trash can. After they ate, they would bring food over to Emily. Nothing made sense. At night, as Benya fell asleep, he would inexplicably have memories of reenacting Brezhnev's funeral as a child.

Emily was clearly changing. When she was awake she walked around with a strange gait. She barely looked at him. She seemed to listen only to Sophia. Her face became dumb. The color in her skin was fading to a sickly gray. She had grown quiet. Sometimes she would fall into a daze and stare right at him with her mouth open. It scared him. Whenever he tried to start a conversation with her, Sophia would intervene and send him back to their room with a nod of her head.

One day, Benya and Emily were alone in her room. Benya was perched on the chair and Emily lay in bed looking at the television. Benya said, "Emily." Her head rolled toward him. Keeping his eyes forward, Benya asked, "How do you feel?" She stayed silent. "What's happening to you?" he asked, quietly enough to blend in with the noise from the TV. "Do you want to leave?"

He looked at her. She had turned back to the television.

Always pay attention to the person who counts sunsets, his aunt Galina had once told him. *It means they know they are dying.*

A day later, Benya found himself sitting in the white van, waiting for Emily to emerge from the bank. *How did I end up here?* His fear felt like nausea. His heart threatened to pop. *How did I get here?* The door of the bank swung open. Emily stepped outside. She was wearing the wig and glasses and carrying a big tan bag. She was walking unsteadily, weighed down to the side. "Go," said Sophia. Benya felt his fear change into a panicked elation.

He put the van in drive and released his foot from the brake; the van inched forward. They stopped in front of Emily, who appeared to be asleep on her feet. Sophia opened the side door. Benya stared. Emily wasn't moving. What the hell was happening?

"Get in the van," said Sophia.

"Get in," said Benya, squeezing the steering wheel and staring over at her.

Emily turned and stumbled back toward the bank like she had forgotten something. She retreated inside. They sat there in silence for a moment. Heat swelled from Benya's stomach to his head. Sophia yelled into the phone, telling Emily to come back out. They waited. Benya looked across the street at Georgy. He was visibly upset. Benya rolled down the window and listened for sirens. He couldn't stop his hand from shaking.

"Fuck, fuck, fuck," said Benya.

"Wait, she'll come out."

"We need to go right now," said Benya.

"Wait."

The door of the bank crashed open and a uniformed security guard ran out. Benya thought the guard was coming for them. He slammed his foot down on the gas pedal and took off down Geary. "No!" screamed Sophia, but it was too late.

"Turn right," said Sophia. "Turn right and go around."

Benya was losing it. He turned right. "Use your signal," said Sophia. "Drive normal, my God, slow down."

Sophia called Georgy on the phone. She was yelling at him in Russian, telling him to stay on her; that they couldn't help it; that the cops were coming.

Benya turned right again onto Euclid. There were people everywhere, heads were turning. "Drive normal," Sophia said again. "Keep going. Go one more block, up there, to that street, Jordan, go right. Go back around. We're dead," she said in English. "We're fucking dead."

They turned back onto Geary. Benya heard sirens wailing, but he couldn't see them yet.

He drove past the bank. He couldn't stop. "Keep going," said Sophia. She was talking on the phone with Georgy. "She's up there, keep going," she said. Benya stole a look in the rearview mirror at Sophia sitting in the seat behind him; she seemed smaller now, she seemed stunned and pale.

Benya drove west down Geary. He saw the blue and red pops of sirens coming at him. He didn't know what to do. "Drive," said Sophia. Police cars were coming from all different directions. "Drive. Georgy's on her. Get us out of here, you idiot."

Benya turned left. Cars slammed on their brakes and honked at him. A taxi driver flipped him off. Suddenly the street became clear of traffic, people, and cops. "Where should I go?"

"Just keep moving. Drive slow. He'll kill us."

Benya didn't know who she was referring to. He was off Geary and away from the bank; for the moment that allowed him to breathe. Would his debt be forgiven, he wondered, if Emily escaped with the money?

Sophia directed him into Golden Gate Park. She was hiding the computer under the backseat. "Take your hat off!" she yelled at him. Benya took the hat and glasses and threw them out of his window. "Why? Why? Why?" she repeated.

Her phone rang.

"Where?" she said into the phone. "No. Where? We'll be right there." She hung up. "He lost her," she said to Benya.

She seemed to almost have a smile on her lips. "Go that way." She pointed Benya straight ahead. "Follow the road out of the park."

They followed Oak to Divisadero and then headed back to Geary; this put them a mile and a half from the bank. Benya looked at the other cars, at the people walking on the street; he looked at the bike riders and marveled at how free they were, how untroubled the rest of the world was.

Georgy stood on the corner waiting for them. Before he got into the van he went to the front and back and removed the license plates. There were different plates underneath.

"What happened?" asked Sophia when he got in. She seemed hysterical.

"She got on the bus. It left before I could get on. I went to my car, but there were too many police. She's on the bus, unconscious by now," said Georgy. It was the most Benya had ever heard him say. Benya repressed a smile. *Fuck these people*, he thought. *I'll get a regular job and pay them back. This is absurd.*

"It's your fault," Georgy said quietly.

"What do we do?" asked Sophia.

"We wait for the bus to turn around and come back. She's not going anywhere."

"We'll go find it," said Sophia.

"There are hundreds of buses out there. She'll come to us," said Georgy.

They parked at Geary and Fillmore. They were only twenty city blocks from the bank.

"We should lose the van," said Benya.

"Don't worry about the van," said Georgy. "Worry about the girl and the money. Throw these into the trash," he said to Benya, holding the two license plates out.

They waited for the 38 Geary bus headed back downtown. Georgy figured it wouldn't take more than thirty minutes for the bus to come back around.

Benya had fallen asleep in the back of the van. He dreamed that Mr. Huang was trying to sell him a shipment of gum. In the dream he sampled the gum, and then tried to pull it out of his mouth, but it wouldn't come out; there was too much of it. Mr. Huang stared at him like he was concerned and patted him on his back.

"Wake up, dear," said Sophia, patting him on the same part of his back. It was dark outside, and quiet and peaceful. Benya was so tired. He sat up.

"Did he find her?"

"No," said Sophia. "We need you to drive to the beach."

Benya rolled his neck to stretch and stepped hunched over to the front of the van. Georgy was already sitting silently in the middle seat. Sophia got out the side door and went into the front passenger seat. The dome light hurt Benya's eyes.

"What are you going to do?" asked Benya. He felt older.

"Just drive out to the beach," said Georgy, pointing west.

"Can you find her?" asked Benya.

"We'll find her," said Sophia. "Don't worry, just drive."

Everyone was calm. They made their way to Fulton and headed for the ocean. Traffic was light. Benya watched the park on his left as he drove. He didn't like how quiet they were being, but he found himself unable to speak. His head hurt. He wanted water.

"Where we going?" he asked in Russian.

"We're meeting someone," said Georgy. "Don't worry."

When they reached the Great Highway, Georgy leaned forward and pointed them into the long parking lot that borders Ocean Beach. There were a few scattered cars, but not many. Georgy directed him down the lot. Finally he said, "Up there, right there," and pointed to a spot.

Benya parked. He turned the engine off. The ocean, black in the distance and white where the waves were breaking, opened out like a valley. The moon was full and lit the beach. Wind blew in from the west. Benya wanted to look back at Georgy, but he was suddenly very scared. Sophia was sitting stone-faced in the passenger seat. She looked apoplectic.

Benya sat up taller so he could see in the rearview mirror. Georgy had turned in his seat, and was looking back at the road behind them. There were cars passing. Benya's eyes went back to the black ocean. A great sadness passed through his mind.

Georgy moved hard from the back and dropped a leather belt over Benya's head and around his neck. He pulled with all his force, leaning into the back of the driver's seat.

It took Benya a second to react. His knees hit the steering wheel. He tried to jam his fingers between the belt and his neck, but he couldn't get any leverage. Georgy was pulling so hard he was grunting. Sophia jumped out of the van and ran away. Benya managed to open his own door, but he couldn't move or call out. He waved his arm around feebly. He found the horn and pressed it. The noise blared.

He felt like they were at a standstill, that surely Georgy would release him now. Georgy pulled harder. Benya's vision started to blur. The grating noise in his ears grew to a loud hum. He punched backward at Georgy, but with no effect. His last thoughts before he died were of Emily and how small the van was.

PART II

4

Emily woke up at dawn, freezing cold. She had no idea where she was. She saw wet leaves and dirt. Her head felt like it had been smashed with a metal pipe. She had experienced many bad mornings in her life, but this was the worst.

She was in the woods. Dirt and woods and trees. The cold was painful, like cuts and burns. Every inch of her body hurt. She knew she was outdoors, but she didn't know where. Her mind turned over images, trying to straighten things out; she tried to trace the night. *How the fuck did I end up here?* The Russian popped into her mind and stayed there like a picture. She remembered his face, she remembered him looking at her. And then there was more.

The hotel, the van, the wig, the redhead, the guard, the cops, the customers; all of these images slowly rolled through her mind. She didn't feel panic yet, just guilt. She felt guilt inside her like she was filled with black tar. She was swimming in it. *What have I done?* She had pointed a gun, she'd stolen, she'd yelled—she had done all these things, including the drugs: the crack, the booze and the pills (*what were the pills?*). She had been made into a slave. She cursed herself in her head until the pain became overwhelming, at which point she cried. Her head pounded; her hands ached with cold. For a few seconds she sobbed into the side of the canvas bag, and then she realized what it was. Her chest tightened with panic. She opened the top of the bag with her cold fingers. It was like a postman's sack: it had a tie on the top that cinched through five holes to keep it closed. She pulled the bag open. There were stacks of bundled money: hundred-dollar bills. She stopped crying.

She got onto her knees and threw up violently. *Where am I?* She was deep in the bushes. Everything around her was still. The sky was beginning to turn a lighter shade of gray, but it looked green. The streetlights made orange circles in the sky. Her head hurt. She was dying of thirst. Her mouth tasted like battery acid.

She patted the bag with her hand to get a sense of the size of it: it was large and full. *Fuck me.* Her face was bunched up in pain; she felt like she had overdosed. It hurt to breathe.

There was another bag handcuffed to her left hand. She fumbled it open with her cold fingers and saw a black wig; under the wig she saw the bomb and the gun. The bomb was blinking red-green. She thought she could hear it ticking. Waves of fear washed through her. She tried to shake the bomb out of the bag, but it wouldn't come out. She put her finger on the wires and was about to pull them, until she became paralyzed by the idea of the bomb exploding. She took the gun in her right hand and pulled the handcuff tight, laid the bag down on the ground so the chain was resting on the dirt, put the gun to the chain, and squeezed the trigger. Nothing. The safety was on. She switched it off and squeezed the trigger again. The gun fired, and her hand jerked back. She hadn't thought about the noise. She held her hand up and the bag was still attached. She had missed. She repeated these actions again. This time she hit the chain, damaging but not breaking it. She was able to work it back and forth until it broke completely, leaving her with the metal bracelet of the handcuff and a few links hanging from her wrist. Her ears rang from the gunshots. She stumbled away from the bomb and the bag, wondering if she was going to die from the pain in her head.

She hurt everywhere. She was covered in dirt and leaves; her clothes were wet. *What fucking clothes am I wearing?* Her memory was murky. Her stomach felt torn open, her legs hurt. With her hand holding the gun in place, she picked up the bag of money and limped out of the bushes toward the street.

She walked along Clement Street toward downtown with the bag slung over her shoulder. Each step was a challenge. The park, where she'd fallen unconscious, was on her left; there were mansion-looking houses on the right. She had never been in this neighborhood. She wasn't even sure she was in San Francisco. A man jogged past without looking at her. She felt like she looked homeless, like her face had finally become homeless looking. She couldn't close her mouth. A childhood memory of three ugly boys yelling *poor, poor, poor* played through her mind.

A few minutes earlier a DeSoto cab had driven past her and now it came back on its way downtown. She stood in the road waving at it. The driver squinted at her and pulled up. The sun had risen.

"Where you going?" asked the driver, looking at her like he couldn't decide if he should take her.

"Take me to a hotel on Lombard," she said. She needed to sleep some more. She needed to sleep and hide. She needed to die from her pain.

The driver took her. He headed over to California Street. She looked at the banks as they passed by, a new kind of dread growing in her. The radio tortured her.

The driver cut through the Presidio and took her to a nondescript motel. She squinted at it, then she bent over the bag and fished out a hundred dollars for the driver and two hundred for the motel. The driver sucked on his teeth and scrutinized the money. He gave her the change. It looked like he was trying to memorize her face.

An Indian manager checked her in at the front desk. He didn't seem to like her. He was hard of hearing and leaned in when she spoke, but away when she didn't. She must have looked poor.

The hotel room was plain, the walls were white, the carpet was blue, and the place smelled vaguely of disinfectant, cigarette smoke, and cinnamon spray. It wasn't as nice as the one the Russians had used, but it was nicer than the one she lived in.

She drank water straight from the tap in the bathroom and then lay down on the bed for ten minutes. A million voices spoke in her head; images came flying in her mind. Then she fell back asleep for another fourteen hours, waking only once to go through the money looking for GPS devices.

When she woke up again it was dark outside. The pain in her head and in her body had gone down, but she still felt miserable. The sound of cars driving by hummed in the room. There was a high-pitched noise, but she couldn't tell if it was electronic or imaginary.

She made sure the blinds were closed and not see-through, then double-checked the lock on the door. She strained to listen for footsteps, but she could only hear the cars and the blood in her head. The money was under the bed; she had to lower herself down to the floor like an old woman to pull it out. She dumped the bag on the table.

Thick stacks of hundred-dollar bills. She had never seen anything like it. It was like the movies. She counted it, then put it back in the bag and hid the bag under the bed: $882,600.

After an hour she brought the bag with her into the bathroom and took a shower. Afterward she looked at herself in the mirror. Her head hurt. Her back hurt. Her gums hurt. Her mind was a train filled with bad memories: beatings, fights, and loneliness.

The next five days were similar to her days at the hotel with the Russians, except instead of being drugged and brainwashed, she detoxed. She began to feel somewhat normal.

She slept fifteen, sixteen hours a day. Each day the same nervous boy came and delivered food from the Dragon Sky restaurant. On the third day she gave him a twenty-dollar tip to go and get her some candy. He brought her bags of it. She drank water and slept. She stayed in bed and watched TV and ate candy.

She thought about her life. She thought about being a child. She had grown up in Sacramento. Her birth mother had been a heroin addict. She had never known her father. She didn't have any sisters or brothers. Her mother died when she was only six years old. She had been raised by a foster mother, a woman named Stacey, who had been a good foster mom; Emily knew she had been lucky that way, but Stacey had died of breast cancer eight years ago, and Emily had never felt any connection to Stacey's husband. There were other foster kids in the house, sometimes as many as five at a time, but Emily didn't feel particularly close to any of them. Not close enough to call and explain her current situation. In terms of family, she was alone.

Emily tried to make sense of her time as a teenager. While she lay there in her hotel room, she tried to look over her years and come to an understanding of how she had ended up on drugs, how she had ended up in the Tenderloin, how she had ended up ripping and roaring all the time. She couldn't find an answer. The feeling of being an outsider was all she could recall. The only feeling she could remember when she looked back at her childhood was pain mixed with boredom.

She found drugs in middle school. First, just alcohol and weed, then mushrooms, acid, ecstasy, and by fifteen she was using heroin and crystal meth. The drugs helped her deal with the pain. By using drugs she made friends. Sacramento was a good place to be a drug-using teenager. She dropped out of high school her junior year. There was nothing there for her. She got a job at a 7-Eleven. She met a boy named Malik, and, when she was nineteen, they moved to San Francisco. He was the first of a string of boyfriends who tried to pimp her out, but she didn't go for it. She'd been in the Tenderloin ever since then. She moved from house to house,

boyfriend to boyfriend, scam to scam. She joined sober pro-
grams and dropped out. She'd get arrested for petty charges,
and would spend a few weeks in jail. Her entire existence
had become centered around trying to get high, but as she
lay in that hotel room, her mind looped through random
memories: she used to go to the library in Sacramento and
read horror stories; she used to draw embarrassing fashion
sketches in a notebook; her friends once surprised her with
a birthday cake; she had been in love with a girl named
Astra; Astra had a dog that wore a handkerchief around
his neck; Emily wanted the three of them to run away, but
they never did.

All these memories didn't help her with her current problem. Emily dialed Pierre's number every day from the phone
in her hotel room. Each time a recording said: *Metro PCS.
The customer you are trying to reach is currently unavailable.
Please try your call again later.*

She didn't know why she was calling him. She told herself
she was through with him. He was violent and vicious and
selfish. He was a bad man. But at least he knew her. He
knew who she was.

She tried to make sense of the Russians. They had used her,
that much was clear. She decided they had probably planned
on either killing her or simply dropping her off unconscious
on some street corner. They probably would have pushed her
out of the van while it was moving. She figured she'd been
given just enough drugs to get her through the bank, and
then what? Did they want her to overdose? Had they wanted
to kill her? She wasn't sure. She was anxious; every little noise
made her sit stone still and stare at the door like a mouse.

What did they know about her? She remembered talking about Pierre at least once in the hotel, but what had she said? Only his name—and Pierre wasn't even his real name. But there was only one Pierre, and he wasn't hard to find. Just go to Sixth Street and ask around. Everybody knew him.

What about herself? What had she said about herself? She had mentioned being born in Sacramento. She had talked about having gone to jail in San Francisco and Alameda. Had she said she lived at the Auburn Hotel? She couldn't remember. Had she said how old she was? Each question brought a new wave of guilt and fear. Why had she talked about herself? She normally didn't go on and on like that. It must have been all the pills they'd been feeding her. She remembered that they had her phone. And they had taken pictures of her. Her body sweated. The television in the hotel room was playing an infomercial about an exercise machine. They had her phone. They had her wallet. They had her California ID card. The address on the card would lead them to a drug program on Treasure Island, but with the phone they could easily get hold of Pierre. *Please don't pay your fucking bill, Pierre.* What would they say to him? He wasn't stupid, he wouldn't just start talking, but still, she had to get over there, she had to warn him, she owed him that much. And besides, Sixth Street was her home. She certainly didn't feel safe here.

She had to do something about the money, too. She sat and stared at the stacks and counted them again. Eighty-eight stacks of hundred-dollar bills. Each stack had a hundred bills, ten thousand dollars a stack. Plus one short stack of what was now twenty-three bills. She couldn't be walking around with all that.

The money was a problem and her head was a problem. She needed some pills. Everything they had given her had worn off. She needed pills. She couldn't think straight. She was hurting. Her head hurt. Her chest hurt. It was like the whole inside of her was fucked-up. She was so scared. She needed some relief. She needed to relax. She vowed in her head that she would not smoke crack, but she needed something, and she was rich now.

She called Jules Gunn from the hotel phone. Jules was a stripper at the Market Street Cinema. She was Emily's best friend. Emily asked her to bring eight thousand one-dollar bills. "Yes, Jules, eight thousand." She told Jules she would pay her sixteen thousand dollars to bring her the eight thousand bills and a bottle of pills. She had to repeat herself a few times and swear it wasn't a joke. "That's one hundred percent profit," she told her. Jules was the only person Emily knew who could do something like that. She was the only friend Emily had who could be trusted. "Don't get followed," Emily said.

Six hours later, Jules pulled up into the parking lot of the motel. Emily snuck out from her room and jumped into the Escalade. Jules looked like an R&B singer in rehab; she was wearing a pink warm-up suit and she had big hair and bright nails. She smelled of perfume. She was pretty, but tore up, too. She kept trying to ask Emily what the hell was going on, and she looked mad every time Emily refused to explain.

"What the hell you need eight thousand ones for?"

"I lost a bet."

"Bullshit."

"Don't worry about it."

"Well, mama is going to worry if her little chicken egg starts doing all kinds of crazy things."

"I know, Jules."

Jules didn't turn her head. She just stared out the Escalade. "And why you at a hotel? Come stay with me."

"I needed to get away."

"Needed to get away. If I didn't know you better, I'd say some man's got you working the track. Where's Pierre's punk ass at?"

"Jules, I'm in a hurry, sweetheart."

Emily gave her the sixteen thousand dollars (unbundled, ruffled and piled in a plastic bag).

"What the fuck is this?" said Jules, looking at the bag.

"It's all there," said Emily.

Jules gave her the pills first, then the money. Emily took a Dilaudid and kissed Jules, who leaned away.

"I'll call you soon," said Emily.

Back at the hotel room, alone again, Emily crushed up another pill and snorted it. She was finally feeling a little bit better. She dumped the one-dollar bills on the bed, checked again to make sure the door was locked and the blinds were closed, and began counting out stacks of ones. She made eighty stacks and slipped the bands off the hundreds and slid them over the small bills. Then she took the hundred-dollar bills and put one on top and one on the bottom of each stack. It was hard to waste all those hundreds, but you had to pay to play. Dummy stacks. It worked on TV. It cost almost twenty-five thousand dollars, but that was all good if it bought you a last ticket out, a backup plan. She filled the bank bag up with the good stacks and stuffed it under the bed. She put the dummy stacks into a pillowcase and jammed that into a closet. Always gotta have a backup plan.

Six days. She had been holed up in this new motel for six days. The only time she'd stepped out of her room (besides with Jules) was to go to the front desk to pay for another couple of nights or to get some toilet paper or plastic cups. She had been too scared and depressed to leave, but she needed to get the hell out of there. She needed to get back to the Tenderloin, back downtown, back to Sixth Street, back to her life. She didn't feel safe in this hotel.

She had to change her look first. She stood at the door and talked herself up until she had the courage to walk to the Walgreens on Lombard. The walk there was a nightmare. She still didn't feel right, and she had left the gun in the hotel. Everything was scaring her. She felt weak, like she had the flu. People seemed to be staring at her. She felt like men were following her. Tall men were standing everywhere, talking on cell phones and looking at her. Every car was an SUV. Every car was a van.

The Walgreens was all bright lights and endless aisles and Filipino women working and tall blond ladies in exercise clothes drinking big bottles of water. The aisles were too small to let anyone pass. She kept bumping into things. She finally found a large black duffel bag and put it on over her shoulder to test it out. The price tag said two-for-one. She grabbed another. She found a black San Francisco Giants jacket, a matching baseball cap, a white T-shirt, and some black sweatpants. She picked up some dark sunglasses and some scissors and paid for it all feeling like she was committing fraud. Even with all the new money, she still felt poor. It was the most she had ever bought in a Walgreens—in fact, it was the most she had ever bought in a store. On the way out she stopped near the door and put on the cap, glasses, and jacket.

Back at the hotel she went into the bathroom and began snipping at her hair. She tried to keep its general girlish shape intact, but it didn't work. She ended up with a short, punkish cut. She looked like a crazy little boy with lady skin. She put on her sunglasses and looked at herself. She put on the hat, lowered the bill down. She looked like one of the dykes who lived at the Auburn; like a little Mexican boy-dyke.

She picked up all the hair from the sink and wrapped it up in a ball of toilet paper and put it into the trash. She put the turtleneck, the blue sweater, and the pants from the Russians into the trash, too. They were hateful clothes. She threw everything into a Dumpster in the parking lot.

She put the hundred-dollar stacks in one duffel bag and the stacks of ones in another. The bags felt equally heavy. She put the empty canvas bank bag in the Dumpster with the clothes and the hair and moved the other trash around to hide it. She drank some water and ate some candy. God bless Jules Gunn, she thought. *God bless Jules Gunn.*

After walking through the room with the Indian manager she was given her cash deposit back. He didn't seem to notice the haircut or the new clothes. He just nodded and nodded.

5

Elias didn't sleep after the Rada Harkov incident. Instead he lay on his couch and let panic grow inside him with every single breath. *Don't leave the body. You should know better. You don't leave the body. It was Trammell's fault. Don't leave the body. Don't leave the body. Don't leave the body.*

He crept into the bedroom and put on black pants and a black hooded sweatshirt while his wife snored in the bed. He found his black gloves in the hallway closet and grabbed some duct tape, his phone, his gun, and his badge. He walked out to his Dodge Nitro and called Trammell. It rang four times and then went to voice mail.

The green clock on the dashboard said it was 5:15 a.m. The sun would rise within the hour. He had to get back to Rada Harkov's house and get her body out before the sun rose. It felt more like a religious fact than a compulsion.

There was no traffic on 101. He drove ninety miles per hour. If they wanted to pull him over, they could. This was a police emergency.

He drove past the airport and called Trammell again: voice mail. *This is Sam, leave a message.* Five twenty-five a.m. Were there cameras on the freeway? Were people awake in Rada Harkov's neighborhood? What if the body had already been discovered? It wasn't out of the question.

He got off on Hillside and forced himself to slow down. As he drove past a deserted mall he wondered if he had reached the upper limit of fear. *Fucking Rada Harkov. Fucking Trammell.* Every traffic light was red; it was maddening, the world had aligned itself against him. A police cruiser drifted by headed in the opposite direction on Hillside. There were people up already delivering the Sunday newspapers.

When he got to Poplar Street he parked in the exact same spot as before. He hit the green talk button on his phone: straight to voice mail.

His door grated when he opened it. He closed the door, but it didn't latch, so he had to lean backward on it. It was 5:37 a.m. It would be a sunny Sunday morning in thirty-three minutes. He walked around the car and covered the front and back plates with duct tape. Birds had begun chirping in all of the trees.

He began to move quietly toward the house. He had his beanie on and his gloves and he was dressed in black and he knew you couldn't choose a more suspicious outfit, but it had to be that way—he had to gamble on not being seen.

Stupid fucking asshole. He turned and hurried back to the Nitro. What was he going to do, carry her body? He had to park in the driveway. He had to. There was nothing to be done about it. *Life is a cold pool*, his father used to say. *You just have to jump in.*

He drove with his lights off past the driveway and then backed into it, parked behind Rada Harkov's car, killed the engine, and surveyed the street. He listened to the sound of the engine cooling down with little clicks. His stomach growled.

If the cops had been there, they certainly hadn't left any sign. The neighborhood was silent. He walked to the back gate; the fence was locked just like last time, only this time he didn't have his little pocketknife. He had taken it off his belt before lying down on the couch. It was 5:42 a.m. If he got caught he would blame everything on Trammell.

CHING-DING-DING-DING. His phone rang out in a flurry of chimes. *Fuck me.* Was it Trammell? He pulled it out. It was his wife, Julie. He could kill her. He could kill her and kill himself. It was all too much.

He pulled himself up and over the wooden fence and landed on the other side with a little thump, then moved straight to the bathroom window. He would have to ruin the toothpaste spackle job he'd done. He didn't have the crowbar with him. He didn't have anything, but somehow he managed to jam his gloved fingers under the window and force it up an inch and then all the way. Legs kicking, he pulled himself headfirst into the bathroom. The shower was still running. The air was cool and humid. The mirror, the walls, the window, everything was fogged and beaded with dampness. He stood and looked in at the body. It was still there, the skin so bright white it looked blue, her hair bright red.

He reached into the shower and turned the water off, trying his hardest to avoid looking at her body. It was horrible. He didn't know if he could do this. The chirping noises coming from the birds outside had grown louder. The sounds of cars driving by the house were coming more frequently.

He stepped to the hallway. Just five hours ago he had been moving through the house with such ease, and now here he was on the verge of a personal breakdown. He needed Trammell.

He found a linen closet and inside it a paisley sheet and walked back to the bathroom, put the sheet on the floor, and bent over and grabbed the woman by the skin under her underarms and pulled her out of the tub. It was the hardest thing he had ever done in his life. It felt like she weighed five hundred pounds. Her skin was white with red splotches. It was horrible. It was hell. The shampoo he had put in her hair seemed like a sick joke.

He pulled her into the hallway and struggled to roll her in the sheet. The arrangement was all wrong, but by now he didn't care. His pants were wet and the floor where he had dragged her was wet, too. All he wanted was to get the hell out. He pushed the sheet under the fleshy part of her arm, but as soon as he moved his hand, the sheet fell away. No matter which way he did it she was always half rolled. He went to the linen closet, his head pounding, and grabbed another blanket and went back to the hallway and threw the blanket down over her and then poked the loose ends under her body like he was tucking her in and then he squeezed his hands under either side of the bundle and lifted her up. It was all blanket and sheets and limbs; it was all legs and arms and fingers and hair.

Strange thoughts passed through his mind while he worked: he thought about a guy he knew in high school who had moved to Los Angeles and become a sports agent, and now posted pictures of himself with beautiful women and apparently drove a new Porsche. He thought of his mother and how her birthday was coming.

He got her up and carried the bundle, wet and heavy, sidestepping as he went, toward the front door, then placed her down on the couch where he and Trammell had sat before they left. Except for one hand with its brown nail polish, and one pink-white-and-blue-fleshed foot, she was covered. He listened. Everything was quiet. His phone said it was 5:54 a.m.

He should have never bet on that Stanford game. If he had bet on San Jose State instead he could have taken the winnings and put them on an over-under the next week. The restaurant he had invested in had been called the Blue Note. Why had he invested in a jazz restaurant? He didn't know anything about jazz or food.

He walked out the front door, carefully closing it behind him, and opened the back of his car. He looked at the houses on the block. They were all 1970s, American-paradise style. They had roofs that sloped up and two-car garages and lawns with grass. A car drove past. The sky was turning brighter by the moment.

He walked back into the house, wrapped his arms around the trunk of the woman's body, picked her up, and walked to the front door. The screen door made a loud metal racket when he kicked it open. He carried her—she was as heavy as a bag of bricks—to the car and dropped her into the back. The blanket and sheet both slipped down and he was confronted with her face, with her lips, nose, and cheeks, but mainly with her dull eyes peeking out through the slits of her dead eyelids. He tried to pull the sheet back into place, but it was pinned under her. He had to roll her all the way off the blanket and onto the floor of the cargo area and then rearrange the blanket to cover her entire body. His hands shook violently.

Back in her room, he rifled through her drawers until he found a pair of sweatpants and a T-shirt. He didn't know what he was going to do with her, but he knew he couldn't have her be naked. He could dress her later; now he had to leave. He threw the clothes in the back with the body and lowered the door and pushed it closed.

Bruce Springsteen, sounding young and confident, was singing on the radio. Elias felt that the world was ending. It hurt to drive so slow. He wished he had cancer. He wished he was a sports agent.

Airport Boulevard. *Where was the damn freeway entrance?* He didn't even see the cop behind him until there was an explosion of red and blue lights in his rearview mirror, and still it took a second to understand that it was a cop. It was a cop and he was a cop. *Calm the fuck down.* He pulled over to the side of the road and breathed in and out. *Calm down. Calm down.*

The officer took a very long time to get out of his cruiser. *Why didn't he put clothes on her?* Things would be easier if she were just fucking dressed. Elias pulled his badge out. He wanted wine, he wanted water. He wanted to reach back and make sure she was still covered, but he knew he couldn't. He waited for the cop.

The officer walked toward the driver's door, holding a flashlight up near his ear, his right hand resting on his gun. *Why was he touching his gun?* Elias's own gun was under the seat; his badge was on his lap. He watched through the mirror, his head not moving, as the officer got closer to the back of the car. The light from the cop's flashlight passed over the cargo area, then shifted toward the front as he stepped forward.

Elias was holding his badge up to the window. The cop, looking very young, skinny, and nervous, stood back at a forty-five-degree angle.

"I'm off-duty and unarmed," called out Elias.

"Who you with?" asked the cop.

"SFPD."

"Let me see it." He was Chinese, maybe twenty-five years old. He took the badge out of Elias's hand like he didn't want their hands to touch.

You don't take another cop's badge, thought Elias.

"Your license, too."

Elias didn't have his wallet. He was dressed in black, head to toe, beanie, hoodie, everything (the gloves, at least, were off). It was not the way to be. He tried to breathe deeply so he could project some kind of calm.

"Listen, I don't have my wallet. It's a long story. My name's Leo Elias, star number 1282, I got my PD ID in there with the badge, call it in, call the station, call Gang Task Force."

"Stand by, sir," said the cop, walking back to his car.

Elias fumed. If they were in San Francisco, he would have kicked his ass. But he had to sit there and take it. His heart was breaking. He couldn't deal. Surely there was a limit to the shit one man was able to endure. The sun was beginning to rise.

The cop came back with fast, loud steps.

"Here you are, Officer Elias," he said, handing him his badge.

"Thanks."

"No problem. Sorry—I had to run you. You know you got your license plate all taped up, right?"

"Shit," said Elias, forcing his face into a stupid smile.

"Why you got it like that?"

"It's my partner's idea of a joke."

"He got you."

"He sure did."

Trammell was sitting on the couch in his living room. His television was on with the volume muted. The screen showed a strong man competition. Huge men were straining as they ran around carrying anvils. Trammell hadn't slept all night.

His phone rang for the fourth time that morning—this time it was Trammell's mother. She called every morning at seven to make sure he was awake.

"Rise and shine, baby," she said when he answered.

"Good morning," he said.

"You up?"

"Of course." One of the men on the television screen dropped an anvil and looked like he was going to cry.

"What time you going to work?" his mother asked.

"I'm off today."

"They still got you on the swing?"

"Yep."

"Better than that night shift, though."

"I said I'm off today, though, Mom."

"But you're still up this early?" she asked, sounding incredulous.

Trammell closed his eyes and saw the dead woman in the shower. He saw her hands, her eyes, her hair.

"It's your aunty Qianna's birthday today," said his mother.

In his mind he saw the woman's car pulling into the driveway. He had called out Elias's name. Where was Elias when he called for him? If Elias had just been there they could have left through the back door.

"You gonna call her?" said his mother.

"Of course, Ma."

"We doing a dinner for her at over at Sandy's."

The woman had been out of the car almost as soon as she had parked. Trammell had committed to staying by the door when he saw her walking. For all he knew she could've had a gun.

"I wish you could be down here for it," said his mother.

"Me, too, Mom," said Trammell.

He hadn't wanted to hurt the lady. He hadn't had a plan at all. He had figured they were going to just talk to her, but by the time she was unlocking the door, Trammell had simply freaked out. His main fear had been that the woman would see his face. He wanted to grab her and then get the hell out, but she started fighting. It all happened so fast. The feeling had been similar to dropping a dish, or getting in a car accident. The events felt drawn in by some kind of force.

"You heard me?" his mom asked.

"What?"

"I wish you could be at this party."

"I said, yeah," said Trammell.

"We thought about doing a surprise party. Can you imagine your aunt?"

"No."

"In the flowers," said his mother.

"What'd you say?"

"I'm talking to Dale," she said. Dale was his mother's husband.

Trammell looked at the television. One of the muscle men was spitting water at the ground and thumping his chest. Trammell closed his eyes and saw the dead woman's face. He saw Elias's ugly face.

"Is your partner still driving you crazy?" asked his mom.

"He's all right," said Trammell.

"So, what are you going to do on your day off?"

"Just go to the gym," he said.

His head hurt. He remembered putting the pillow over the woman's face. The memory seemed detached, like he had watched someone else do it. He did it to help her. He remembered putting the gun to her neck.

"You still dating that Shirley?"

"Nope. Not really," he said. He knew he sounded flat.

"She was nice, though."

"Mom."

"You could've brought her down to Qi-Qi's party."

A memory of his aunt Qianna catching him and his cousin masturbating passed through his mind; her face had shown confusion and then sympathy.

"Just saying," said his mother.

"Tell her happy birthday for me."

"You said *you'd* call her."

* * *

McLaren Park was a perfect place for this kind of madness. It would be empty. It would be secluded. It was a regular place to dump bodies.

University Street dead-ended near Mansell. There was a steep, woody hill with houses to the east and the park with its trees and bushes to the west. It was a residential area, but there wasn't much foot traffic. It would do fine until dark. He could come back later with Trammell and deal with her properly, but right now, at this moment, the only thing Elias needed to do was separate himself from the body.

He parked the car at the end of the block. He went to the back and opened up the door. The body was still covered with the blanket.

A memory of camping played in his mind. His father used to take him to Yosemite in the summers. They would fish.

He laid her clothes out; her sweatpants were stained with specks of white paint. Was he losing his mind? His hand shook as he pulled the blanket off her. The worst was her dead face. *I need a new life*, he thought. *I need a new job.*

Get her dressed. He looked up the block again and then started pulling the shirt over her head, but it didn't work—it went over the head, but the arms didn't fit into the arm holes. Her body had become stiff with rigor mortis. It was like a puzzle. *Do it*, he told himself, *like a living person would, arms first.* He pulled the shirt over her cold hand, trying not to breathe any smells, and then he got the other arm in and pulled the shirt up and over her head. The pants were no easier. *Fuck, fuck, fuck.*

Her back arched like a board as he lowered her legs out of the car. He put the blanket over her head and upper body and dragged her from the car to the wooded area. She was bundled up in the blankets and he bear-hugged her body close to his and her feet dragged in the middle of his steps. He took her to the steep side, away from the trail. The sun was shining and there were planes in the sky. He put the body down about a hundred feet away from the street and rearranged the blanket and sheet to cover her. *The mafia robbed a bank*, he thought, *they robbed a bank, killed the manager, and dumped her body in the park.*

Elias went from the park to a corner store on San Bruno and Bacon, bought an eleven-dollar screw-topped bottle of Chardonnay and a thirty-two-ounce mango-flavored Gatorade, went outside, took a sip from the Gatorade, then bent down and dumped the rest in the gutter. He then poured the wine into the empty bottle. An old Chinese woman, collecting recycling out of a trash can on the corner, turned and walked away from him when he tried to give her the empty wine bottle. He went back into the store for oranges, but they didn't have any. He had to settle for some kind of chocolate-cake thing for his breath.

Trammell lived on Topeka Avenue; Elias figured he would just casually drop by. It was 7:10 a.m. Trammell should be up by now. He took his phone out to see if his partner had called. There was a voice mail message from his wife. He texted her while he drove: STILL WORKING.

Elias parked across from Trammell's house. The block was silent. The houses were drab. Trammell was one of the only cops who still lived in San Francisco. Elias drank wine from the Gatorade bottle and chewed the chocolate cake and stared at Trammell's door wondering whether he should even tell him about moving the body. He didn't want to scare him. He was sure Trammell would be in a bad mood. He'd have to treat him with kid gloves.

He pressed the little white doorbell. A car drove by. He couldn't hear whether the bell had sounded, so he leaned in a little and pressed it again. This time he heard a dull buzz. He could see into the kitchen, but that was all. He waited. He was so tired. He pressed the bell again, giving it the little one-two, one-two rhythm of a friendly call. Nothing. The house was silent. He took out his cell phone. It rang five times and then went to voice mail.

"Hey, Sam, what's up, it's Leo. Hey, I'm right outside, man. I just rang your doorbell—we gotta talk. Listen, why don't you just call me when you're up and we'll meet up and talk about our work stuff, you know. Okay, cool. Thanks, partner." The word *partner* came out sounding pinched, like Elias had run out of breath.

He walked down the stairs and toward his car. When he was in the middle of the street he turned and saw the blinds on the living room window swinging.

This thing was moving fast. No time for sleep. He had to catch them now. Had to find the money. *Thanks, part-ner.* He did the math in his head: the bank got robbed on Monday, today was Sunday—Monday, Tuesday, Wednesday,

Thursday, Friday, Saturday, Sunday, seven days. *Find the girl, solve the case, get the money.*

The Hall of Justice was big and gray and deserted looking. Elias parked on Bryant Street instead of in the lot and, because he was trying to avoid his coworkers, went in the front door like a regular person, instead of the side, like a cop. He nodded to the young sheriff's trainee who was manning the door, and even in this little gesture Elias felt inauthentic. He kept repeating the nod as he waited for the elevator.

His cell phone buzzed. He looked at it; a text from his wife: LETTER FROM BANK. CALL ME.

When he went into his office, one of his co-officers, Cal Toomey, exactly the type of person he was trying to avoid, looked at him and said, "Jesus, Leo, what the fuck happened to you?"

"Just working."

"You look like shit," he said, then, his voice rising almost to a shout, "Fucking man in black here." He turned his head and called out to someone in the back, "Hey Dickhead, come look at fucking Plastic Face, the man in black, working on a fucking Sunday." He turned back to Elias. "You looking to make sergeant, or what? Fucking shithead."

"Shut up!" yelled Elias.

He went to his desk and turned on his computer and leaned back in his chair, feeling as tired as he ever had. As the computer hummed to life, his hands went down to his pockets and he realized he didn't have what he was looking for. It felt like a jolt. He wanted to scream. He didn't have the phone numbers they'd gleaned from Rada Harkov's phone. He didn't have Sophia's number. Trammell had the numbers. He wanted to bang his head on his keyboard. Nothing was working. *Okay, think, think . . . Stanford, San Jose State, Blue Note . . .* and it came to him like a song, *610, Joe Montana, 49'ers:* 610-1649. He wrote it down on scratch paper and logged onto his person-locator program.

The phone was a Sprint cellular phone registered to Sophia Kamenka. 2516 Fifteenth Avenue, San Francisco. Elias smiled for what felt like the first time in his life.

"Sophia Ka . . . menko." Cal Toomey was standing behind Elias's shoulder, bent over and spying. Elias nearly screamed. "What the fuck? You stalking her?" said Toomey.

"Fuck you!"

"Fuck me? You're dressed in black stalking a Polack lady on your off day. I should fucking arrest you. Fuck me? Fuck you, you fucking sicko."

"Not the fucking day for this."

"All right, come on, hands up, up against the wall." Toomey started to wrestle with Elias, grabbing at his wrists.

"Fuck off!"

"Jesus, Leo! What's wrong with you?" said Toomey, looking like his feelings were hurt.

"I'm busy," said Elias. He was using his body to shield the monitor from Toomey, who decided the game was over. He walked away with his fat swaying walk, his chest puffed out like a pigeon.

Elias took a pen and wrote the address onto a piece of paper. *15th Ave, 15th Ave, 15th Ave.* He'd run her criminal history later. On his way out he could have sworn he heard Cal Toomey saying the words *McLaren Park.*

Trammell still hadn't slept. It was almost 10 a.m. He had started drinking screwdrivers after getting off the phone with his mom and he had continued drinking even as Elias had come to his door and left.

Why the fuck did God put me with you? Trammell wondered. *God could have partnered me with any other cop, but he chose you: crazy fucking Plastic Face. Fucking psycho. Probably punishing me for choosing to be a cop. Ugly motherfucker. Fuck you, God. Fuck you, Plastic Face.*

The ice in the screwdriver had melted into little almond-shaped spheres. Trammell looked over his living room. A thin coat of black dust covered the floor. His house was near both freeways, and dust from the tires of cars had invaded every surface.

I should have never become a cop, thought Trammell. *I'll quit. I'll put in my two weeks' notice and quit. Move back to L.A. Work with my hands. Be a chef. God doesn't like cops.*

Trammell had often daydreamed about becoming a chef. He imagined that cooking food brought a kind of professional contentedness that he could never find by being a cop. Food made people happy. He wanted to open a pizza place.

Move back and open a pizza place. He imagined throwing the dough. *Call it: Love Triangles.* He saw the dough in the air, and then he saw the redheaded woman. He saw her hair thrashing around while he was trying to get a hold of her.

He saw her laid out on the ground. He saw the shell of her body, a body that had been alive, and was now dead.

He saw his aunt Qianna. He saw his mother. He saw Elias.

He fell asleep and dreamed that he was in a museum in Chicago. He was playing basketball on the third floor. He was shooting three-pointers in a wide-open space. He was making the shots. A worker came and told him it cost thirty dollars to be in there. He told the worker that was robbery and then they argued about who was more poor.

Her house was on a nice little hill in the Sunset District. Elias parked across the street, a few doors down, and watched.

It didn't look like a bank robber's house. It had an orange, Spanish-looking roof, clean white walls, a big bay window with white-lacy blinds. The small yard was filled with well-tended plants. The window in the living room probably had a view of the ocean. There were no cars parked out front.

He watched the house, feeling sleep, hunger, thirst, and the need to piss in equal measures. He didn't have a plan—he would go to the door and see what he saw. If somebody was home and they challenged him, he would improvise, ask for Mr. so-and-so, something like that. He would wing it.

He walked up the stairs to the front door. Everything had become more vivid: the orange of the stairs, the brightness of the blue sky. The doorbell sounded out in a series of low-toned gongs. He felt as though he were being watched. Nobody answered. He rang again. Butterflies grew in his stomach. A low-pitched sound reached his ears. He looked around and tried to read the meaning of things. A garden hose, rolled up with cobwebs on it, was sitting near his feet. Do bank robbers water their plants?

He looked over his shoulder and then reached in through the metal gate to the mailbox and pulled out two pieces of mail. The envelopes were addressed to Sophia Kamenka.

He went back to the car and watched. Nothing was happening, nothing was moving, nobody was coming or going. It was Sunday—*where were they?* His AM radio guys talked about sports. He liked the way they yelled about things: everything was black-and-white; everything was figured out.

A sheriff's deputy pulled out Billy Franco from his cell and brought him into an interview room. It was another long shot, but Elias had run out of ideas.

The deputy opened the door to the tiny room and asked Elias if he wanted Franco in cuffs.

"Nah, he's all right," said Elias.

Franco was in an orange jailhouse uniform. He looked like he needed some sun. He was withdrawing from something; he looked unsteady, and had a raw sore on his temple. He appeared to have just woken up.

Elias took a stick of Old Spice and set it on the table. After pornography, deodorant was the second most valuable legal commodity in the jail.

"What the fuck y'all pulling me out for?" said Franco, taking the deodorant and tucking it into the front waistband of his pants.

"It's not *y'all*, it's just *me*."

"I'm on the mainline, man—you understand? You can't just pull me out—y'all gonna get this motherfucker killed in here."

"Tell them it was your lawyer," said Elias.

"On a Sunday? Come on, now. So, what you want, Plastic Man?" said Franco, looking over his shoulder at the window on the door to make sure none of his fellow inmates were walking by. There was dandruff in Franco's black hair.

"There was a bank robbery in the Richmond."

"So what?"

"So what do you know?"

"I know it happened."

"What else?"

"That's it, man. I read it in the papers."

"You know any Russians?"

"Are you kidding me?" He looked incredulous. Hostile.

"Come on, *Franco knows all*, remember?" said Elias.

"Not this one."

"Well, this is the one you want to know," said Elias. "This is no joke." He leaned across the table and whispered, "Find me something good and I'll get you out of here."

"Good like what?"

"Russians," said Elias. "Find us some Russians. Russians doing anything. Ear to the street."

"Man, my ear works better when I'm on the street," said Franco.

"Give me something."

"What do I get for something?" asked Franco. He didn't seem happy.

"Consideration," said Elias. "Serious and good consideration. And a call to your parole officer." Elias watched for a reaction, didn't see one, and continued: "Garcia's my buddy. He's my cousin's husband." The cousin's husband stuff was a lie, but he had the right parole officer: Franco's eyes squinted.

A group of inmates dressed in orange walked by the interview room pushing food carts. Franco let them walk ten steps past and then he stood up, put his head out of the room, and yelled to the deputy, "Hey Caldwell, man, take me away from this punk motherfucker unless he's ready to charge me with something."

He turned back to Elias and asked, "You at the same number?"

"Sure am," said Elias. "Call me collect."

"We'll see," said Franco.

6

"Give me a quarter piece for a hundred," said Emily.

"Damn, girl, slow down."

"I'm in a hurry."

"That don't make you God here," said Pros, looking past her and down the street. Pros was a teenage Cambodian boy. Leavenworth Street, between Turk and Eddy, in the center of the Tenderloin, was where he held court.

Emily preferred to buy marijuana from him, or his cousins. They had the best customer service, they were consistent, and because Emily's boyfriend, Pierre, was friends with their uncles, she never got ripped off. This was the first stop she made after returning to the Tenderloin.

"Y'all on some cop shit, or something?" said Pros. He wore a baggy white T-shirt, a black pea coat, a beanie, and baggy jeans. His face was scarred by chicken pox.

"Say what?"

"Man, they was on you."

"What the fuck you talking about?" asked Emily.

"Last time you were here. Two white niggas was following you in a white van. Man, y'all went on some state's evidence shit."

Emily thought about the last time she'd tried to buy from him. It was right before she had met the Russian. She had asked and the boy had said, "No," just like that, "No," and then he'd walked away from her. It had pissed her off. She'd gone straight to the bar after that, and then she'd met the Russian. She tried to make sense of what the boy was saying, but she couldn't.

"They were following me?"

"Hell yeah."

"Who?"

"In a white van—it was all bad," said Pros, shaking his head.

"When?"

"Like I said, last time I saw you."

She tried to think through the problem. They had been following her before she met the Russian. It didn't matter what it meant; she didn't care. She didn't come here to learn the history of who was following her. "Give me a hund sack—"

"And that ain't even it," the boy said, cutting her off. "Yesterday some other white dude came here like he *knew me*. Showed me a picture of you and said she ain't in no trouble, woo woo woo, then he took a hundred-dollar bill, ripped it in half, gave me half, and told me if I saw you and called him he'd give me the other half." He dug in his pocket and produced one half of a hundred-dollar bill. Then he pulled out his cell phone and said, "Should I call him?"

"No," said Emily. "Shut up."

Pros was a little drunk. His eyes were red and his breath smelled like cognac. He put the phone away and said, "You know I wouldn't do you like that. You my older sister." He handed her the torn bill. Written on it was "Emily 415.610.1822."

"What'd he look like?" asked Emily.

"He looked like a military nigga, but he talked like a Terminator."

"Was he older? Brown hair?" asked Emily, trying to describe the Russian.

"Nah, he was a little wiry dude, with short buzzed hair and a face like he was hella cold, eyes all bugged out—hella cutty."

Emily remembered the ugly man.

"They got the wrong girl," said Emily, shaking her head in confusion.

"Come on," said Pros. A youngster opened the gate of the apartment building, and they stepped into the entryway. There were four young boys sitting on the stairs leading up to the front door. Emily put her two bags, which held almost a million dollars, down by her feet. Nearly thirty years of hustling had taught her that the safest way to act was to act like she didn't care.

Pros leaned into her and whispered, "So you really want a quarter for a hundred and twenty?"

"I said a hundred."

"My boy could do it right now."

"Then do it, my nigga."

Pros said something in Cambodian and one of the kids ran up the stairs into the apartment building. "It's gonna take a little minute. Walk with me," he said. Emily picked up her bags and they walked back out onto the street.

"They putting up all kinds of most-wanted posters for your ass. They on some Wild West shit. You fucked up."

"It's not me," was all Emily could think to say.

"But you're famous now."

Pros got distracted by a car he knew and tried to wave it down. Emily had a moment to collect herself. She pulled her hat down and attempted to compose herself.

Pros came back from the car and led Emily up the street to the corner. He pointed at a light pole. Taped to the pole was a flyer with a black-and-white photo of her face. She had a vague memory of the flash going off. *Say cheese.* It had been taken at the hotel. Her face in the photo was slack, and she was looking just left of the lens. The words below the photo said: *Emily Rosario is missing. Her family must talk with her. Please call 415.610.1822 if you see her. $1,000 reward for information leading to her location. Emily is 5'3", 110 lbs, she has black hair. She is 31 years old. Thank you. Emily Rosario Family Rescue Counsel.*

"What the fuck you do?" asked Pros.

"Nothing," said Emily, looking around to make sure nobody was watching her, which, with hundreds of people out on the street, cars driving by, and five stories of apartment buildings on all sides, was hard to guarantee. She reached up to the pole and ripped the thing down.

Pros led her back into the entryway of 245 Leavenworth.

"What you got in your bags?"

"Nothing."

"Why'd you cut your hair?"

"Why you think, stupid."

"Man, y'all better get the fuck out of town," he said. "Get your ass to Richmond or Sacto, outta state somewhere."

"I'm about to."

"What's Pierre got to say about all this?"

"He knows I'm good."

"Man, y'all better tuck your tail and run."

"It ain't like that."

Emily felt small. She wanted the kid to return with her weed. How did she know the kid wasn't going to call the Russians himself? How long was he going to take?

"When did they put those up?" she asked, trying her best to look bored.

"After they came asking about you."

"Did you take them down?"

"Hell yeah, I took 'em down, but they had some bum put 'em back up the next day."

"Let me see your phone," said Emily.

He handed her his phone and she dialed the number. The call went straight to voice mail. A Russian-sounding woman's voice said: "*Thank you for calling the Emily Rosario Family Rescue Counsel. Please leave a detailed message and a telephone number where you may be reached. If your information leads to the reunification of the Rosario family, you will win your reward. No questions asked. Thank you.*" Emily hung up.

The kid came back downstairs and handed Emily a paper bindle filled with a quarter ounce of weed. She sniffed at it.

"Damn, y'all ain't got no bags?" she said.

"We out," said the kid.

She didn't open the bindle. It felt solid in her hand. She handed Pros a hundred-dollar bill and he checked it against the entryway light.

"All right then," she said. She picked up her two bags.

"Careful, shorty," said Pros. He opened the metal gate, scanned the block, and made way for her.

Sixth Street was crowded with people buying and selling crack and pills. Everyone owed someone. Everyone was bored. A few people were smiling. A ghostly-looking white guy with hollowed-out cheeks walked by with a chair on top of his head. Two black guys passed after that, one of them hurrying the other, saying, "Come on, man, come on."

Emily walked on the far side of the street and looked down the Minna Street alley, toward the Auburn Hotel. Nothing appeared out of the ordinary, but she knew better than to stop. The front door was not an option. She hid behind her sunglasses and hat and scanned the faces of everyone who walked by her. Everyone was a potential enemy. Everyone had gray faces and looked angry. Nobody spoke to her. The gun in her pocket made her feel something she had never felt before—not safe, necessarily, but she felt bigger.

She went to the Kingsley Hotel, where a black guy was manning the desk, which was nothing more than a box protected by a cage of thick metal, like a fence. There was a little slot to talk through and Emily stepped up to it, scanning the sign-in sheet on the desk. Somebody had visited a man named Lawrence Pope in room 402.

"I'm here to see Mr. Pope, four-oh-two," she said.

"ID," said the man at the desk.

Emily pulled out a twenty, slipped it through the slot, and told the man she had lost her ID.

He looked at the money and nodded his head toward the stairs.

The hotel was quiet except for the sound of competing televisions. It smelled like ammonia, sweat, and cigarettes. There were smudges of white rice stuck in the carpet and grime marks on the walls. Everything was dirty. Emily took the stairs two at a time. A sign on the door to the roof said, NO WALKING. ALARM! She ignored it and pushed the door open.

Outside the air was cool and windy. The fog was orange in the sky. There wasn't anybody out there. She crossed the tar-papered roof and headed toward the Auburn. She felt dread and fear, but she also felt comfort to be back in the Tenderloin; she knew how to move through this place, she knew the currents and eddies.

The two roofs were nearly the same height. She hopped down to the Auburn and headed to the roof door, which was unlocked. She opened it slowly. Her stomach felt scared. She felt scared all over. She wondered if she should have accepted Jules Gunn's invitation to stay with her. The bags were so heavy. She wished she could hold the gun in her hand instead of in her pocket. The stairs were dark, the building hummed.

She could hear a man yelling about the unfairness of something. He had a raspy voice, and he sounded drunk. The third floor was filled with noises and smells. She walked as quietly as she could toward her room. The rug, which she had never really noticed before, was burgundy. Near the end of the hallway she came to her door. She went toward it, trying her best to sense any danger. She walked like a hunter, rolling her heel to the ball of her foot and lifting up gently.

A door of a different room snapped open and a man she didn't know staggered out of the room and headed toward her. He looked Arab. Like a druggy Arab. She tensed up, but he ignored her and went to the stairs.

She put her ear to her door and listened. She couldn't hear anything. What if Pierre was sitting in there? What could she say to him? *Look, man, I'm rich, pack your bags, people are after me.* She didn't want him to come with her, though. She was through with him. But she wanted to warn him.

She stepped past her door to the next one down and knocked gently. A man named Isaac lived there. He yelled out, asking who it was. Emily winced and looked behind her. She knocked again, louder.

The door opened a crack and Isaac peered out at her. "Pierre's been looking for you," he said.

"Can I come in?"

"You got any dope?"

"Come on, man," she whispered.

He pulled the door open a little wider and stuck his head out to see if she was alone. He was a big white man with thin greasy hair and thick glasses. His room was filled with scraps of things, metal and furniture and taken-apart televisions. He collected things. It made a small room smaller. She had to squeeze past him to get in. The room smelled like rust. The sheets needed to be washed.

"You leaving?" he asked, looking at her two bags.

"Coming back."

"Pierre's looking for you."

"Where is he?"

"Haven't seen him," he said. "You got any dope?"

"No."

"You got your hair cut," he said, looking at the sides under her hat.

"Yeah."

"All fashionable." He had a southern accent, even though he was from Fresno. "Can I borrow some money?" he asked. She looked at him. Did he know? He didn't, but he could smell it.

"I'll loan you a twenty in a minute," she said. "I gotta go out your window."

"Lost your keys?"

She moved to the window.

"That cop down there been coming by, too," he said, stepping behind her and pointing out the window and down into the alley.

Emily looked where he was pointing. There was a silver car parked in the alley, across the street from the front door of their building. She couldn't see inside the car, just the roof and the hood. It didn't look like a cop's car.

"Why's he a cop?" she asked.

"'Cause he's a white guy, keeps coming by and knocking."

"How long's he been there?"

"Last couple of days. I thought he was Pierre's parole agent, but then he asks me one time if I seen you." Isaac smiled; his teeth were brown and gapped.

She stared down at the car wondering who it was.

"Why don't you leave them bags here," said Isaac, pointing down at the floor. "Go round, unlock your place, come back and grab 'em?" He flashed the same smile, looked from the bag to her eyes and back again.

"You wanna borrow a twenty?" she asked, ringing a tone that suggested the twenty may be at risk. He snorted and turned away.

She squeezed out the window onto a little grated fire escape and pulled the bags out after her. It was acrobic; sweat appeared on her forehead and under her shirt.

Her window was just a few steps from Isaac's; she went to it slowly and looked in. Nobody was in there, but Pierre's collection of videos was scattered on the floor.

She looked down at the silver car, which was directly under her and across the alley, and then she pushed her fingers under the unlocked window and pulled up; it opened noisily.

"It's open," she whispered back toward Isaac.

"You got the twenty?" he said, his head and body sticking out of the window.

"Hold on," she said. "Go back in your room."

She climbed into her room. The videos had been knocked off their shelf and onto the ground. Pierre was a neat freak. The military made him that way. He would never leave his videos on the ground. She sniffed at the air. She could smell a trace of Pierre and a trace of cologne. It felt wrong in there. She went to the door and made sure it was locked, and then walked to the window and checked on the car.

Where could she hide the money? Their room was so bare it would stick out anywhere. She looked up at the ceiling. It had a push-away dropped ceiling like an office. They had stashed drugs up there before. Would it hold the weight of the bags? She grabbed a chair and got onto it, but she couldn't reach the tiles.

She got back down. If she could just get rid of the damn bags—that was all she wanted, just to be free of the bags for a minute. Isaac was calling for her. She went to the window. "Shut the fuck up," she hissed.

She went into her pants pockets and found a twenty and pushed herself back out the window, looked down at the silver car, and scooted over to him.

He was hunched down near the window with his face all bunched up. "I gotta leave in a minute," he said, like an apology.

"Here," she said, holding out the twenty. "Now shut up. And don't tell nobody you saw me."

"What about Pierre?" he asked.

"You can tell him. Tell him I'm trying to find him."

"Well, you could come back out through here when you leave," he said, gesturing toward his room. "Just lock it from behind."

She scanned the room. Isaac backed away from the window and pulled on his jacket. "I'll be back later," he said, and he left.

An idea occurred to her. She went back into her room and opened the two bags of money. She took the dummy bag, hid it under her bed, and set the mattress back down over it and did a kind of mental chant to stamp it in her head: *dummy bag, dummy bag, dummy bag.* She put on a black jacket from her closet and transferred the gun and weed into the jacket. She grabbed the bag with the real money, checked the silver car, and went back out the window and into Isaac's room.

Isaac was gone. She could reach the ceiling in here. She looked around his cramped room and found a chair covered in clothes. She rearranged the clothes and labored to bring the chair to a desk. After moving the collection of books and magazines from the desk, and setting them on the ground, she put the chair on the desk. She climbed up onto it and pushed the ceiling panel away. She got back down and opened the bag and took one of the bundles of hundreds and put it in her back pants pocket, then zipped the bag closed. The bag was heavy, but she pulled it to the ceiling and pushed it up into the darkness. It held. She replaced the ceiling panel, got back down, replaced the books and magazines, and examined everything. She moved the chair back where it had been and covered it with the clothes. *Boo-ya.*

The roof was the only place Emily felt safe. She sat up there, on the edge overlooking Minna, and watched for Pierre. She watched the car in the alley. The sun had set. Fog was pushing in. Traffic noise was blowing all around. She smoked her weed and organized her thoughts.

They were looking for her. They were not going to stop looking, and even if it felt better to be on Sixth Street, it wasn't safe. She played with the idea of leaving with Pierre, but nothing about it felt right. He had laid his hands on her. The idea of leaving alone felt even worse, though. She felt an intense physical wave of loneliness. She didn't know where she could go. San Francisco was the only place she knew, and even if all of her friends here were junkies, they were still her friends. California felt like its own country, and leaving it felt like volunteering to be homeless. She thought of Jules Gunn, and a wave of shyness passed through her.

A red light flashed below her. It was the brake light from the silver car. It lit up once and then went off. *All right, fuck face,* she thought, *you wanna come to my block and try and stalk me? Then we gonna see what's up with your ass.*

"Hey, Muhammad, let me borrow that phone real quick," said Emily.

The store clerk, Muhammad, looked at her and then behind her at everyone else in the store. "This ain't a phone booth," he said.

"Damn, cousin, let me use it, a girl's in trouble, I gotta call nine-one-one," said Emily, puffing her chest out.

A man pushed past Emily and asked for three scratchers. Muhammad rang the man up and then handed Emily a black cordless phone. "Stay here with it."

She dialed the phone.

"Nine-one-one emergency," a voice said.

"Yeah, can you send a cop," said Emily, turning her back to the clerk and stepping aside to let a woman pay for a can of beer.

"What's the nature of your emergency?" said the operator.

"A woman is being attacked," said Emily.

"Okay, ma'am, where are you calling from?"

"I'm at Sixth and Howard, but I saw this a block up at Sixth and Minna, on Minna in front of the Auburn Hotel."

"What hotel?"

"Minna Street, between Sixth and Fifth; it's an alley."

"What did the suspect look like?"

"He was in a vehicle. In a silver parked car."

"Okay, what was his race?"

"Don't know, didn't see him, but I bet he's a white Caucasian."

"What was he doing?"

"He's sitting parked on Minna."

"What type of vehicle, ma'am?"

"I couldn't see, but I saw him hitting a girl. She looked like she might be a student or something."

"Okay, what race was the girl?"

"She was trying to get out. It was bad, send help, I gotta go." Emily hung up and handed the phone back to Muhammad.

"Why you lie to them?" he asked.

Emily walked up Sixth Street with her hands in her pockets and her hood over her head. The gun was in her jacket pocket. She felt keenly awake. When she reached Minna she leaned against the wall near some winos and waited. *This is my block.*

Ten minutes later a black-and-white patrol car turned left onto Minna and slowly drove toward Fifth Street. Sixty feet in its red and blue lights popped on. Two cops stepped out.

The one who'd been driving went and stood behind the silver car. The other one walked onto the sidewalk and pulled out a flashlight and shined it into the car.

The officer spoke with the man inside and then appeared to take some identification from him. He stepped back and called something in on his chest radio.

Emily watched the cop disappear back into his squad car. After a few minutes he walked back, bent down to the driver's window, and handed the guy his license. They talked for a few seconds and then the cop returned to his own car.

Emily moved from the corner and trotted along the wall. She was scared, but she also felt an anger that seemed to carry her along. The cop car rolled away. The silver car was parked facing away from her so she was coming at it from the back. She could see the shape of a man in the driver's seat.

Emily jammed the gun in through the man's open window. He flinched back and Emily reached in with her free hand and clicked the unlock button on the door. She jumped into the backseat.

He was a bald man with a thick neck. He struggled against his seat belt, trying to lean away from the gun. "All right, all right," he said, leaning forward.

"Sit up, asshole. Hands on the wheel. Sit up or I'm gonna blow your fucking head off." Emily was surprised at the sound of her voice. "Roll your window up."

The man reached for the window button and pressed it. Nothing happened. "Okay," he said, "I have to turn the car on to put the window up." His voice sounded pinched.

"Turn it on. Roll it up."

"Okay, all right. I'm reaching with my right hand for the key. I'm turning the key."

"Shut up!" said Emily.

"Turning the key." The man was obviously scared. He seemed to be in his fifties, and he had an American accent, not a Russian one. He was shaking. He turned the car's electrical power on and rolled up his window. The car beeped. Emily looked behind her; the alley was empty. She started to second-guess herself.

"What the fuck you doing here?" asked Emily. Her mouth was dry.

"Nothing," said the man.

"Bullshit, cracker motherfucker—what the fuck you doing in this alley? Put your hands on the wheel."

The man put his hands from his head to the wheel.

"Take the keys out," said Emily. He took them out. "Now, I'm going to ask one more time, what are you doing here?"

"I'm a private investigator." The man tried to turn his head to look at her, but Emily put the muzzle of the gun against his ear.

"Don't turn. Go on."

"I'm a private investigator. Please don't hurt me. I'm just working. I'm a good guy."

"Bullshit. Good guys don't sit in alleys. What are you doing?"

"I work for King Insurance. I'm working on a case."

"What case? Talk fast, asshole."

"I'm here investigating a bank robbery."

"You a cop?"

"I told you, I'm a PI."

"Give me your wallet."

The man reached for his wallet on the seat next to him and handed it back to her. A car drove past them down the alley. Emily, her eyes going up and down from the wallet to the man, managed to fish out a license and a business card. She held the card up so she could read it and keep an eye on him at the same time. The card read: Timothy Nichols, WWW Investigations, 1001 Lakeview Rd, Sacramento, CA.

"Okay, mister, listen to me Mr. Motherfucking Nichols," said Emily, looking over her shoulder and then slumping down in the seat. "Listen to me good: you've got one chance to save your life or I will pull this trigger, so help me God. I've done it before, and I'll do it again." Emily waited for him to reply but he was silent, so she continued. "Begin from the beginning and tell me everything. And I know why you're here so don't fuck with me."

"All right," began Nichols, "all right. No problem. I'm from Sacramento. I work for King Insurance."

"The card says WWW."

"King, I subcontract from King Insurance."

"What are you doing"

"Okay, there was a robbery. I got a call on Tuesday to come to the city and look at it. Just a formality. It's just an insurance thing. Like a—function—"

"I don't care about all that," she said, pressing the gun to the back of his head. "Tell me why you're parked here."

"Okay, no problem—look." The man tried to steady his breath. "Robbery. I came out. I looked at the video with the manager, the bank manager, I talked with the police inspector, we talked, that's it. I promise."

"Why are you in this alley?" said Emily. Her lips were smacking when she spoke. She needed water.

"I'm here—I sent my report to Los Angeles, my boss, the insurance man. I wrote it. I sent it."

"So, what's the bank robbery, what happened? What'd you say?"

"I said what the police report said: a lone female comes into the bank and walks up to the manager and hands her a phone. Wig, glasses. Walks out with the money. Case still open."

"So what the fuck are you doing here? I'm not playing with you. How'd you end up parked right here?"

"I followed the bank manager. All signs pointed to her."

"Talk faster," said Emily. She was high and she couldn't understand what he was saying, but whatever it was, she wanted him to say it faster.

"I'm telling you. I'm telling you how I got here. The manager was in on it—"

"You said that, go on."

"I followed her. She met with another lady and guy."

Now Emily was interested. "Go on," she said.

"I followed them."

"Who?"

"The new lady and man."

"Who were they?"

"Russians."

"And what'd they do?" asked Emily.

"They drove around in a van for a few days and they kept coming here."

"Why?"

"I don't know."

"And why'd you stay here?"

"See what they wanted."

"What'd they want?"

"To find the lone female."

"Liar."

"I didn't say it was you."

"It's not me, asshole."

"I'm just saying I was sitting here wondering when this lone female was going to arrive."

"Man, you're in over your motherfucking bald-ass head."

"I didn't say it was you." He sounded like he might cry.

"It's not me, motherfucker, get it? But I got a friend who was in his room and now he's missing, probably with his fingers all broken out. All right? And I got a true suspicion to believe it's because these so-called Russians did it."

"We should call the cops."

"No," said Emily, touching the gun to the back of his head again. "We ain't gonna call no fuckin' cops to come here and do this and that. Give me that paper." She pointed the gun at a manila file on the front passenger seat.

Nichols leaned over and picked up the file and handed it back to her.

She looked through it, her eyes going from the man to the paper and back again.

"What do we have here?" Emily read from the notes. "Emily Rosario, DOB 1/11/83. SS #572-65-9275. Anthony Baptiste = Pierre. 3/18/70. 580 Minna #312." She looked out the back window to make sure nobody was sneaking up. "Well, aren't you a little cocksucker? You gotta be so smart—and you gotta lie like a motherfucker, too."

PATRICK HOFFMAN

"I didn't lie," said Nichols.

"Well, you forgot to mention Emily Rosario."

"I didn't want to scare you."

"Why would that scare me?"

"I don't know." Nichols shook his head. "I don't know anything."

"And you got the room number?"

"I paid some lady to follow them up."

"Follow who?"

"The Russians."

"And why I am I supposed to believe it wasn't you in the van out here doing too much?"

"'Cause I'm cooperating. I didn't bother anyone."

"So why they coming here?"

"They want their money."

Emily stayed silent for a moment. She didn't know what she should do with this information. Her head hurt. Her heart was pounding. She just wanted to find Pierre, so she could leave.

"If you want, I'll pack up right now and just go back to Sacramento and call it a day." He tried to peek back in the mirror at her.

"Where's Pierre?"

"I don't know."

"And who's Emily?" she asked.

"She shares the room with Baptiste, with Pierre."

"Well, Mr. Look-at-me-all-smart-over-here, she's got nothing to do with this, so just forget about that bitch," said Emily.

"Done."

"Go be smart on your own ass time."

"Listen," said Nichols, "we have the same goal. Whoever you are, your enemy is my enemy. We're friends. I don't know who you are—but I just gave you some valuable information. So as long as you've done nothing wrong, no reason to start now."

What was he saying? She was having a hard time listening and thinking at the same time.

"You gonna run to the cops?" she asked.

"I'm private. I don't even like cops."

"You gonna share this information with the cops?"

"No way."

"You gonna share it with your damn insurance boss."

"I don't know a single thing about it."

"And that's how it's going to stay."

"Whatever you want."

"All right. Here's the deal. I don't like making threats on no one; I don't like telling people what to do"—she tapped the gun against the back of his head—"but it's time for your ass to leave San Francisco. And it's time for you to forget everything you've been learning on your little fact-finding mission. Next time I see you, I'm gonna kill you."

Emily got out. She walked back toward Sixth Street with her eyes on the car. When she got around the corner she stuck her head back around to look. The car was dark except for the red taillight. *He's still got his foot on the brake,* she thought. *He's a lying motherfucker, too.*

7

Sophia Kamenka moved through each room in Rada Harkov's home and tried to make sense of what she was seeing. She found the linen closet open, with sheets spilling out; she found the wineglass on the counter; in the hallway, a picture frame was tilted ominously off center. There were traces of a puddle on the bathroom floor. The window showed signs of forced entry.

Rada Harkov, the bank manager, was Sophia's niece, her brother's only daughter, and the only thing in Sophia's life that didn't seem soiled. Now she was missing. For the past two days every phone call had gone unanswered. She was gone. Hatred twisted in Sophia's chest and guilt swelled in her belly. *Yakov Radionovich,* she repeated his name in her head: *Yakov Radionovich.*

Twelve years ago Sophia had convinced her niece to move from Tel Aviv, where she had been living, to the United States. Sophia had promised it was better here. She had promised that Rada—incorruptible, smart, sweet Rada— would be able to make something of herself. This, she had told her, was a place where you could get ahead. And Rada had. She had gone back to school, gotten a degree from an American university, a job, promotions, married, and divorced. She had gotten a house—this house.

Sophia sat down in her niece's bedroom, as her thoughts, like glaciers, slowly fell into place; her guilt was complete and total. Images of Yakov Radionovich, his bald head, his sagging, mole-covered face, kept appearing in her mind.

For years Rada Harkov's position as manager of the bank had been a nagging temptation to Sophia. Every time Rada mentioned the bank, even in passing, Sophia's mind would drift toward thoughts of stealing. Rada would talk about work, and Sophia would nod her head as though she were listening, but inside she would be thinking, *You're the manager of a bank. How can you not want to rob it?*

Rada would have never agreed to it. They both came from a family of criminals, but Rada had long ago aligned herself with the normal life. When Rada was a child, her father, Ivan, used to joke that Rada's red hair and pale skin marked her as a law-abiding citizen. He had been right.

And Rada would have happily remained in the normal life if Sophia hadn't made the mistake of doing business with Yakov Radionovich. Both Sophia and Radionovich shared connections with a larger crime syndicate based in Brooklyn, and led by a man named Vadim Vertov. Sophia and Radionovich's relationship with each other had always been tense. Both felt that they alone should be in control of Vadim Vertov's San Francisco business ventures. On occasion they were forced to work together, usually when drugs were involved; but for the better part of a decade they had been allowed to operate independently. Sophia believed that

Radionovich was too stupid to run such a large operation; he was also, in her opinion, needlessly violent. Radionovich, for his part, still could not accept a woman as his equal, and Sophia knew that he believed that she was not capable of the kind of violence necessary for the mafia life.

Two months ago Sophia had made arrangements to sell forty pounds of crystal meth to an associate in Southern California. The drugs were supplied to her by Radionovich's gang with the understanding that payment would come after the deal was complete. The man Sophia chose to deliver the drugs had been arrested outside Modesto by the California Highway Patrol. The drugs had been seized.

Radionovich used the occasion to pounce. He'd arranged a meeting at his teahouse, and within minutes of her showing up he'd begun haranguing her. Sophia didn't understand where his anger was coming from; losing drugs was a natural risk of dealing drugs—she would pay him back—but Radionovich was acting as though this were the first time someone had been arrested. "My money," she remembered him saying; "it is my money that you lost."

"So, what do you want me to do?" she had asked.

Radionovich's face had been red. She remembered him licking his upper and lower lips before he next spoke: "Your niece's bank," he'd said. "Take out a loan."

Sophia, sitting in Rada's bedroom, tried to remember how the conversation had played out. She remembered feeling a sense of depression at the prospect of bringing Rada into this, but if that were truly the case, why hadn't she refused the idea right from the start? She remembered Radionovich making vague threats: "Well, if you cannot pay, we have other ways of dealing with it." But that wasn't it, either.

There was a part of her that knew she had been willing to go along with Radionovich's suggestion, but right now, sitting on her missing niece's bed, she was not ready to examine this willingness; instead she let her hatred of Radionovich take full bloom. She sat in Rada's bedroom and hated the man with all her soul.

Her mind went back to the meeting: "She will never agree to it," Sophia had said.

"She will if I don't give her a choice," Radionovich had answered.

And that had been the moment when she could have stopped it all; she could have demanded that they bring the debate to Vadim Vertov to settle. In reality it was a small amount of money; she could have moved some assets around and paid Radionovich off within the week. So why had she agreed to go forward? Because Radionovich had been testing her mettle; he had been trying to bait her into going to Vertov, so instead of doing what he wanted she chose to act out of pride. She called his bluff and now her niece was missing.

The rough outlines of the plan had been hashed out over the next few days. Radionovich would confront Sophia in front of her niece; he would demand she make payments on her debt. Sophia knew that Rada would never agree to rob the bank if the plan was brought to her; she had to be under the impression that it was her own idea.

An encounter was arranged. Sophia took her niece to dinner in the Richmond. The restaurant, Russian and formal, was owned by one of Radionovich's associates. As they were finishing their meal, the establishment cleared of patrons. The waiters casually disappeared to the back. Radionovich, Georgy, and two other men came into the place and sat down around their table.

"You enjoyed your meal?" Radionovich asked in Russian.

"It was exceptional," said Sophia, trying to act casual.

"You tried the fried liver?"

"Yakov, you know me too well."

"And you, my dear," said Radionovich, turning to Rada, "how is the bank?"

Rada looked toward Sophia, hoping she would answer for her, but when Sophia remained silent, Rada answered that the bank was fine.

"What a beautiful thing," said Radionovich, looking at the two of them sitting at the table. "An aunt and her niece enjoying a nice dinner." The mood at the table shifted.

"Please, not here," said Sophia.

"Here is where I found you," said Radionovich, the words rolling over mucus in his throat.

"Listen to me, I will come to you and we will talk later," said Sophia, gesturing like she wanted to get up from the table. Georgy stood up, blocking her exit.

"You know your aunt is a real magician," said Radionovich, moving his hands as he spoke. "She appears and disappears whenever she wants."

Sophia remained silent. Rada stared down at the table.

"You owe us," said Radionovich.

"Please, this is not the place."

Georgy, still standing, walked behind Rada and began massaging her shoulders. "Don't be so tense," he whispered in her ear in English. Rada blanched and stared at her aunt.

"Perhaps your niece can arrange a loan," said Radionovich. The seed was planted.

Sophia felt sick with guilt as this memory played through her mind. How had she let this happen? How had she been so stupid? Of all the wretched things she had done in her life, and there were many, this was the worst. She tried to convince herself that Radionovich had made her do it: *he made me*, she thought, but it wasn't true.

Less than a week after the encounter at the restaurant, Sophia finally pretended to give in to her niece's offers of help. If Rada agreed to help her get out of this one situation, Sophia had said, she would never involve her again. And so they decided to rob the bank.

The plan, created by Sophia herself, was designed so that neither Sophia nor Radionovich would have any direct tie to it. Sophia would find an American girl, a drug addict. The fact that she was American would help distance them from the crime. They would control the girl with drugs: crack and oxycodone to lure her in and keep her settled; a mixture of scopolamine, Estazolam, and amobarbital to break her will.

Radionovich said he could supply a man, a Russian named Benya Stavitsky, to serve as the handler. Stavitsky was desperate and would do exactly as they told him. If he got caught, no problem. If he died, no problem. He was disposable.

Things fell apart almost immediately. It became clear within the first few hours that Benya Stavitsky would not be up to the task. He could not be counted on; he was depressed, and helpless. Within minutes of arriving at the hotel he was smoking crack. He could not handle himself, let alone the American girl. Besides, it was not in Sophia's DNA to relinquish control. The plan had been orchestrated to ensure that Sophia did not have any contact with the American girl, but shortly after getting Emily to the hotel, Sophia knew she would have to take over. After the first day it became clear that Sophia was on her own. Benya Stavitsky was no help to her; even Georgy—except for his ability to make a credible bomb and his silly little cameras—proved useless.

Sophia was not supposed to ever go to the bank. She was not even supposed to be in the area. Benya Stavitsky was supposed to handle the job, with Georgy following. Now Benya Stavitsky was dead, the drug-addicted American had somehow stolen the money, and Sophia's only family, her little *kulkoka moya*, was missing.

Just a few days ago Rada had called Sophia from a pay phone and told her that Radionovich had come by her house. She had insisted that he did not threaten her, that he only wanted to hear her version of events, but for Sophia, the fact that he visited her proved his guilt. She sat on her niece's bed and tried to calm her fear. If anything happened to Rada she would kill every last person involved. *Surely, he must be holding her until the money is found; he'll return her after that.* He must have taken her as some type of insurance policy; it was unthinkable that he would have harmed her. Whatever the case, it was an act of war. *They will all meet the devil. I will cut off their hands. They will all be buried in the earth.*

Her thoughts were interrupted by her phone vibrating harshly in her pocket. She looked at the phone and saw it was Radionovich's man, Timothy Nichols. Nichols was an American that Radionovich used to find people. He had been stationed outside Emily's apartment for the last few days.

"Yes?" answered Sophia.

"I just met your girl," said the voice on the other line.

Sophia, thinking for a moment that he was talking about her niece, then understanding it was Emily, growled, "Where is she?"

"She's standing at the corner of Sixth and Minna watching me."

Sophia closed her eyes for a moment and tried to picture the scene: the image of Emily staring at Nichols while he spoke on the phone seemed absurd.

"Follow her, idiot."

"Don't worry."

"Don't worry? Why didn't you stop her?" asked Sophia.

"'Cause she had a pistol pointed at my head."

"You're at the Auburn?"

"That's right."

"Georgy will be there in five minutes."

8

A few hours before Sophia received the call from the American telling her he had seen Emily, Elias had walked into the Gang Task Force office and found Trammell standing with six other cops in front of a dry-erase board. It had been one day since Elias moved Rada Harkov's dead body and he still hadn't been able to tell Trammell about it.

Trammell had seen him come into the room. Their eyes met for a moment, but Trammell looked away. Elias flanked the group on the right side and tried again to catch Trammell's eye, and again was ignored. It was preposterous. Why in the hell would he ignore him at a time like this? Elias's stomach was beginning to hurt in a way that felt medical. Trammell could not have seemed further away. Elias felt a deep loneliness.

"Hey," said a cop named Oscar Tulafona, coming out of nowhere.

"What?" said Elias.

"You fucking stink." He said it hatefully.

Things got worse. As the meeting ended, Sergeant Muniz came into the room and called Trammell over to him.

Trammell joined the sergeant at the doorway for a moment; they conferred with their heads down and their hands up near their chins, like a pitcher talking to a manager, and then they stepped out of the room. Where were they going? Elias looked around to see if anyone else had noticed. Nobody had. They were all joking about something. Everyone was carrying on, laughing and joking. Their skin looked horrible—a sea of pink skin and broken capillaries. Fat. They were all fat. Everyone was joking and fat. The room was closing in on him. He needed a drink. He needed to talk with Trammell. Make sure he was going to stay solid.

Trammell was gone for what felt like an hour. An hour of panic. The worst hour of Elias's life. Was Trammell confessing? Elias couldn't breathe. He was sweating. He pretended to write a report. Where was his partner? Trammell could save him with a few kind words. *Where is my partner?* He could imagine two scenarios and both were equally bad. Either Trammell was snitching on Elias to save himself, telling them everything about the redhead, the bank, everything, or he was trying to get some kind of transfer, trying to save himself that way. He was trying to leave. That was clear. He would snitch his way out, or he would beg his way out. Elias knew it. In the end, friends weren't friends, they were enemies.

Elias tried to read Trammell's face when the man stepped back into the room. Trammell was ice cold. He always had been. He was a fake. That was the thing about him, that's why he was so successful, that was the reason why everyone loved him. He was a fucking fake.

"Let's go," said Trammell. His face looked sad. Elias got up from his desk and wondered what that sad face could mean. *Did he snitch? Did he snitch?* Sadness and fear fought for majority control of Elias's inner self.

They walked silently to the car, Trammell staying a few paces ahead of Elias. *He's acting like I killed that lady,* thought Elias. A nasty feeling filled Elias. He wanted to ignore him, but he couldn't. He couldn't stop paying attention to him. He was transfixed. He couldn't think one thought that didn't relate in some way to Trammell. He couldn't even stop looking at him. He measured his back and wondered whether he could take him in a fight. He knew he couldn't.

They got in the car. Elias got in the driver's seat out of habit, but he didn't know whether he was able to drive. He was so tired. He hadn't slept in over fifty hours. They sat in the car without moving.

"How are you?" Elias finally asked, not knowing what else to say. His voice came out dully from the top of his chest; the sound of the words echoed around the car. He had to physically will himself not to cry. He could smell his own breath.

"I'm good."

"You need anything, you let me know, right?"

"Course," said Trammell. Just that single, disdainful word: *course.* Elias turned and looked at him. It looked like all of Trammell's facial muscles had bunched up into a genuine mask of hatred—a hate mask. His skin, normally brown, looked gray. The whites of his eyes were bloodshot. Trammell snorted through his nose and looked ahead. None of it seemed genuine. He seemed like a different guy. Like a complete stranger.

"What was the sergeant saying?"

"Nothing."

Nothing. Nothing. Nothing.

Elias almost got into an accident as he pulled out onto Seventh Street. A truck honked and lurched. Trammell's hand shot up to the ceiling. Elias felt like he needed to be 5150'd. He felt shaken.

They drove in silence. Elias debated with himself until finally he said, "I found the Sophia woman."

"Uh huh," said Trammell.

The Federal Building grew taller as they approached it. A labor union was staging a protest in front of it. "No union! No peace! No union! No peace!"

"She lives in the Sunset," said Elias. He didn't know why he was telling Trammell this, but he couldn't stop.

Trammell stayed silent. They crossed Market Street.

"Super-normal house, garden hoses," said Elias. He didn't even know what he was saying anymore. He couldn't stop talking. "Nice house. It looked like medium rich. Weird."

Trammell rolled down his window and said, "I don't know what the fuck you're talking about."

"Just working," said Elias, defensively. And just like that he was burning. His face was red. He didn't know why. He wanted an excuse to pull over so he could drink wine. *What was I talking about? What was I talking about? Fuck you.*

Elias drove up Leavenworth in silence. This was rock bottom. He was driving in a city filled with junkies and bums, driving around with a murderer, and he had to defend himself. He silently mouthed the words *fuck you*.

The police radio was droning on in the background. Elias felt seized by panic every time he heard mention of the Ingleside District. He was convinced the dispatcher would be calling out an 802, code for a dead body, at any moment.

He decided it would be better not to tell Trammell he had moved the body. Better to let him think she was still sitting inside the house.

They drove in silence, circling through the Tenderloin, causing people to shout out "Five-O!" on every block.

After a while Trammell quietly asked: "Did you hear anything?"

"What?"

"Did they find her yet?"

"The girl?"

"The lady," said Trammell. "The lady at the house."

Is he bugged? Is he wearing a mic? Did they put him up to this? thought Elias.

"I don't know what you're talking about," said Elias. He couldn't think. He couldn't come up with the right words. He couldn't even understand what Trammell was asking. He kept driving. His mouth became dry.

"Did they find her?" asked Trammell again.

"Who?"

"The cops," said Trammell. "The cops? San Bruno?"

Elias heard the words and weighed them. "The girl you killed?" he asked. It came out too hard. It was a test. He wanted to test Trammell, see if he was bugged.

"I didn't kill anybody," said Trammell

Elias looked at him and felt confused. Trammell continued staring straight ahead. *Didn't kill anybody.*

Elias turned left onto Eddy Street and then circled back around on Polk. A tranny prostitute blew him a kiss. There were crowds of homeless people.

"I can't work," said Elias.

"Me neither," said Trammell, and this small agreement, this tiny little coming together, made Elias feel something like hope. He wanted to reach out and hold Trammell's hand. He wanted to be close to him. He wanted to smell him.

Elias's phone rang in his pocket. The caller ID said San Francisco County Jail. A recorded voice told Elias the call was collect from an inmate. He pressed 1 to accept. It was Billy Franco, the snitch.

"I got some good news."

"What?" said Elias. The tiredness, the depression, it all disappeared.

"I found what you wanted."

"Tell it."

"You gonna help me?" asked Franco.

"Of course." *Course. Course. Course.*

"You gonna get me out of here?"

"Of course." Elias knew the call would have been recorded, but he didn't care. "Tell me," he said impatiently. He looked over at Trammell, whose face had morphed back from ugly to beautiful.

"Apparently, some Russians have been looking for a girl called Emily Rosario. They want her bad."

"Consider yourself a free man," said Elias.

"When you gonna get me out?"

"Whenever you want."

* * *

"We got her," said Elias; his smile, an unsure, painful-looking thing, seemed to be asking for a response, for some kind of affirmation, but Trammell didn't know how to respond. "We got that bitch," said Elias. "Emily Rosario, stealing my money, stealing our money."

Trammell's face looked confused.

"I pulled our snitch Franco out of CJ-5 and asked him to work his magic," continued Elias, "and boom." He raised his cell phone to show Trammell. "Fucking got her. She's the one. We got her. Billy Franco's in the fucking house, dog!"

If Trammell smiled while Elias told him this, it wasn't because he was happy; it was because he was scared of Elias, who had gone from listless to crazed in the span of a phone call. Elias's behavior wasn't just unpredictable, it wasn't a mood swing, it seemed mentally unstable. Trammell's smile was a reaction to this instability. It was the type of smile offered to appease a crazy person.

Elias raced through traffic to get them back to the Hall of Justice. Trammell followed him into the building. He wanted to keep him in his sight, make sure he didn't do anything stupid. Elias went straight to the Identification Bureau and ordered Emily Rosario's most recent mug shot.

Back in the hallway they looked at the page, her picture on the right, her description on the left. She had been arrested ten months earlier after trying to buy oxycodone from an undercover cop. The picture showed Emily in the county-issued orange jail suit. Her face looked vaguely hopeful, like she expected to be released after the picture was taken. Her skin was pale. Her hair had been long then; it hung down past her ears. She was five feet three inches tall and weighed only one hundred and twenty pounds. Tattoos: *Bildad*, left wrist; *Champion of the World*, left shoulder; clear complexion. Her last known address was 480 Minna Street, 312, San Francisco. Elias recognized the address as the Auburn Hotel.

"We got this fucking bitch," said Elias, nodding his head as he drove them back to Sixth Street. They drove past the Auburn and parked about fifty feet from the front door. The alley was quiet.

They had to buzz at the front gate to be let in.

"Who you here to see?" said the manager.

"Parole sweep," said Elias, flashing his badge. The manager, his face looking indifferent and tired, buzzed them through the second gate.

They went up the three flights of stairs, passing a young woman smoking a cigarette who called out after them, "Hey Darryl, here they come! Whoop, whoop!"

Nobody answered at Emily Rosario's door.

Emily's neighbor, Isaac, tucked inside his room, listened to the banging and wondered what all the fuss was about.

On the way back out, the manager confirmed that Emily Rosario did in fact live there.

"Y'all know me by the swag of my walk," sang Elias as they walked back out into the night. "The swag of my talk, the swag of my block."

He opened the door to the car, looked at Trammell, circled with his finger to the sky, and said, "She's here, I can feel her." He raised his eyebrows and asked: "You wanna fish for her here? Or should we circle?"

Trammell shook his head.

"Let's circle."

They did loops: Leavenworth to Sutter to Hyde to Eighth to Folsom to Sixth and back again. They looked at every female they passed on the street, measured their bodies, mentally weighed them, took in their height, their race, and tried to match them to their image of Emily Rosario. They decided not to use any more snitches at this point; better to keep the circle small. "She will appear," said Elias. "They always do."

Elias told a story about finding a murder suspect named Dante Hayes, who had been particularly hard to track down. It was from back when Elias still worked in the Ingleside District. Trammell had heard it before but he played along and nodded when he was supposed to. "Must have checked his house over twenty times," said Elias. "Finally caught him at the YMCA on Ocean. Welch was working out, spotted Dante lifting weights." Elias looked at Trammell, who nodded. Elias continued: "Wanted for murder, but still had to get his workout in." Elias laughed. "I told him when I cuffed him that he could lift all the weights he wanted at San Quentin."

It was well into nighttime now. There were cars filled with kids from the suburbs coming into South of Market to hit the clubs. Homeless men were trying to wave people into parking spots. People smoked cigarettes on corners and people smoked crack in doorways. Massage parlors sat open next to liquor stores. Men and women gathered in small groups on corners.

Later, when he was interviewed about what happened next, Elias would lie and tell the inspectors that he and Trammell had been on their way to the Henry Hotel in search of a gang member named Duda Rue. He would say they were just parking when they had spotted Emily running; in reality, they were driving back to Emily's apartment when Trammell spotted her. He noticed her walking across Sixth Street close to the wall. "Whoa, whoa, slow down," he said. Something about the way she walked, the fact that she was wearing a hat, her size, her race, her coloring all matched, but it was something more than that, something that couldn't be quantified.

"Hold on, hold on," he said. Elias stopped and Trammell jumped out of the car and crossed Sixth Street against traffic. Elias didn't know what was going on. He turned in his seat and watched and debated whether he should back up, turn around, or jump out. He decided to jump out. Emily kept walking away from them toward Howard Street.

Elias ran a few steps and then shadowed Trammell from across the street. He felt scared; his heart was racing. His hand kept going down to the gun at his waist. Sixth Street was crowded with people; the buildings were tight and tall, and there were no alleys to run through. There was a group of young Chinese kids lined up to get into a club.

When Emily looked behind her and saw Trammell coming after her, her first thought was that he was making a mistake, maybe confusing her for someone else. He wasn't Russian. The idea that he might be a cop was just starting to form in her head when she bumped square into Elias.

PATRICK HOFFMAN

"Hey," said Elias, like he was trying to wake her up. She had walked into his chest. They were in the middle of Sixth Street. Cars were stopping and honking. She tried to step around him, but he grabbed her shoulders and held her.

At first Emily thought he was trying to help her. "I'm okay," she said, pulling her arm away. His hand tightened on her wrist. She looked into his face and saw ugliness and hatred; he looked like he might hit her. Even dressed in plain clothes, she could tell he was a cop.

"I'm all right," she tried again.

"Come on," said Elias, pulling her toward the curb. Emily's eyes darted around at all the cars, all the people; nobody was helping, everyone was either staring or ignoring her, but nobody was stepping forward to help.

Trammell caught up to them and took her other arm, knocking into her, making her lose her footing for a second. They pulled her up and toward the sidewalk.

"Nah," said Emily. She tried to pull her arms away, but they both held tight.

Her mind raced. They were cops, she could tell by their faces, but what were they stopping her for?

"I didn't do nothing," she said. Her mind wheeled around.

They pushed her toward a big blue building. Her heart raced. She looked around for help, but the sidewalk had become deserted; every window was empty.

They kept her moving until the back of her head hit the wall. Were they cops? Were they with the Russians?

Elias held up the mug shot and looked from it to her face and back again. "It's her," he said.

Emily winced. *If I could take it back*, she thought. *If I had stayed on the roof.* She wanted to cry. *If I stayed at the hotel.*

Trammell held her tighter, the expression on his face, to Emily, appearing incomprehensibly hostile; if they were cops, why were they so mad?

"You fucking bitch," said Elias. "You know how long we been looking for you?" He pulled his hand back like he was going to hit her. She flinched, and the back of her head hit the wall behind her again. He got right in her face, his expression even worse. "We're trying to save you," he said. His breath was hot and bad.

"What's your name?" asked Trammell.

"Mariah," said Emily.

Elias swung her around so that her face was toward the wall. She stared at the grout between the bricks; she stared at the texture of the brick and tried to organize a plan. He began patting her down. His hands were rough on her.

"You need a lady cop to search me!" said Emily.

He groped around her pants. Her fear, expanding inside her, felt like it could lift her up. *Why didn't I leave town?*

"What the fuck we got here?" he said, finding the gun in her jacket pocket.

"That's not mine," said Emily, looking back at him. Trammell tightened his grip on her shoulder and pushed it into the wall. Elias popped the clip out of the gun, confirmed it was loaded, popped the clip back in, and put the gun into his jacket pocket. During the entire investigation that came later, an investigation that included hundreds of officers, this gun was never discovered; it sat untouched and unnoted in

Elias's pocket even as he was questioned by the homicide inspectors.

Cars were driving past like nothing was happening.

He jammed his hands into her pants pockets and found the bag of marijuana. He pulled it out, looked at it, sniffed it, and handed it to Trammell.

"My God," he said. "You're fucked."

None of this mattered to Emily. She didn't care about a gun charge, or a weed charge, but the fact that they were looking for her, the fact that they were carrying around her mug shot, seemed to mean they had her for the bank. That fucking PI, he probably called them as soon as she left.

Elias found the bottle of Dilaudid and shook it. His lips were smacking like a cokehead. Emily could hear him breathing heavy. He moved down her legs and found the stack of hundred-dollar bills tucked into her sock. Everyone got quiet. Trammell smiled.

"Keep it," said Emily. "Just fucking keep it."

"Keep it?" said Elias, looking at Trammell. "She wants us to take a bribe."

"She's a gangster," said Trammell.

"What do you think?" asked Elias.

"I think she'd get ten years for the gun, plus two for the pills, and one for the bribery of a peace officer." He pulled out a radio, turned his back to them, and spoke into it. All of the problems that Trammell and Elias had been having disappeared like fog. They felt awake. They felt free. They felt strong.

"Bullshit," said Emily. "That shit ain't even my gun."

"What about the money?" asked Elias.

A man walked by, skirting around the parked cars. Emily thought about yelling for help, but decided against it.

"I found that. Swear on my mother. Right up on Turk Street," she said.

"You found a stack of hundreds on Turk Street?"

"I know," she said.

Trammell was still forcing her right shoulder into the wall. She couldn't move.

"You sure it wasn't on Geary?" asked Elias.

"What?"

"On Geary?"

"Nah, on Turk," she said.

"Not on Geary?" asked Elias again.

"Not at a bank on Geary?" asked Trammell.

Emily felt sweat on her forehead. Dread boiled in her guts.

The two cops stepped even closer to her, jamming her up against the wall like they were going to rob her. She braced herself for a beating. She could smell sweat and alcohol. The older one needed to shave and he didn't seem stable. She turned her shoulder, pushed her knee against the wall, and tried to squeeze through them.

"Hold on there," said Elias. He elbowed her back against the wall and reached under her shirt with his left hand and grabbed the skin of her stomach and pinched it. "Hold on," he said. Emily tried to push his hand away, but his wrist was like a metal bar. Her skin felt like it might tear. She wanted to cry out, but she couldn't.

"Shhh," said Elias in her ear. "Did you get it at a bank?"

"Hell no," she said.

Elias let go of her skin and held the mug shot up to her face. "You see this?"

"So what?" said Emily.

He took the paper away from her face, leaned in, and said, "Where's the money?" His breath smelled alcoholic. It smelled sour. The stubble on his face was gray; the whites of his eyes looked yellow. His skin was dry.

Emily was dying of thirst. There was no good thing that could come from this. This was it.

Trammell loosened his hold on her shoulder, moved closer to her, and spoke into her ear: "Look, we got you with a gun, you got drugs, you got money on you that was stolen from a bank—"

Emily opened her mouth to speak, but was cut off.

"You got bills with serial numbers that match stolen bills from a bank. We got video. We got DNA at the bank. You're fucked. It's over. Chowchilla time. You gonna be a hard-ass bitch."

Elias leaned in and spoke calmly. "Now, the way it's going to go down is this: you're going to tell us where the money is, and we'll let you go." He looked at Trammell.

"Scot-free," said Trammell.

Elias whispered, "Listen, we are the only people that know it was you, but in about two minutes, I'm going to call in and tell them that I've got the girl who robbed the bank. It doesn't matter if you think we can't prove it. We can. We have video, you have the money. It's over. Unless you give us the rest of the money, and we forget about your stupid junky ass, and everyone goes back to their happy ways."

They waited. A cloud of depression moved in. Emily didn't know what to do. She had never experienced not knowing what to do in such a pure way. Her insides were splitting. It felt like her heart was breaking. She wanted to shut down, she wanted to go silent on them, maybe even fall down onto the street, let them prove whatever they had to prove. They seemed like they might kill her. She was too scared to think. Time crawled. People were walking by now, but they weren't doing anything. *Where is Pierre?* Emily watched as a white van turned the corner from Howard onto Sixth Street. It drove past them. She looked at the driver. He was staring back at her. It was the ugly Russian man, the quiet one from the hotel. Their eyes locked as he went by. "They got it," she said pointing at the van. She felt anger inside.

"Who?" said Elias.

"Right there in that van, the Russians."

Elias and Trammell both watched the van as it continued down Sixth Street and then turned right onto Minna. The two cops exchanged looks. Something shifted. The word *Russians* echoed in the moment. They pushed Emily in front of them and began walking toward Minna. People sank back to let them pass. Everyone stole looks at Emily to see if she was snitching. *Fuck all y'all*, she thought. Minna was four hundred feet in front of them. They walked without speaking. As they approached the corner, Trammell let go of Emily's arm and hustled ahead. He peered around and then looked back at Elias. "It's sitting right there," he said.

"They got it," said Emily again. "They got the money." She didn't know why she was saying it. It felt compulsive.

She couldn't control her words. She said it calmly but with conviction. The words came out hot. Maybe they would let her go.

"Let's go," said Elias, pulling her by both arms. When they turned the corner Emily saw the white van idling in the middle of the alley. It wasn't parked, it just sat there, about two hundred yards in. Elias pushed her forward. The alley was clear of people. It got darker as they went. Emily looked for the PI's car, but it was gone. Sirens blared down Sixth Street, headed for some other incident.

The cops pushed Emily toward the wall of the alley. Before she knew what was happening the white one was lifting her right hand and handcuffing it to an iron window bar. He was breathing heavy like men do before a fight.

"No, you don't got to do all that," said Emily. He clicked the cuffs closed.

Elias nodded his head toward the van, and said, "Go."

Trammell began trotting with his gun out toward the van. Elias followed right behind. Emily pulled on her hand, trying to yank it free. The cuff bit into the skin of her wrist. The city sounded like bees in her ears. She was lost.

As the cops got near the van, the engine shut off. Emily watched as the taillight went dark. She watched as Trammell jogged forward. The driver's side door of the van popped open, and the man Georgy stepped out. Emily watched as he walked toward Trammell. They were about twenty feet apart from each other. Georgy's posture was straight, and he seemed perfectly relaxed. He had a slight smile on his face. For a moment Emily thought they might start talking to each other. They were ten feet apart. Emily watched as Georgy's right arm raised up. Everything slowed down. The next thing Emily saw was Trammell's head snapping back like he had been punched. The color red floated in the air. And then she heard the unmistakable sound of a gunshot. Trammell fell backward. Shot in the head.

Emily watched the other cop shoot. She saw the Russian man's head explode. It only took one second, and then everything was over. Two men had been shot dead right in front of Emily's eyes. It happened as fast as someone clapping their hands twice.

She yanked on her hand again, but it wouldn't budge. She said, "No, no, no," and "Fuck me," but nobody was there. Elias bent down and checked his partner, then walked over to the Russian and looked down at him. He went to the driver's door and looked into the van and got into it. Emily experienced a brief moment of hope—she thought he might drive away—but then the back doors of the van swung open and Elias jumped out.

He walked straight toward her. She tried to find the strength to scream, but she didn't have the breath. She was suffocating. There was nothing she could do. She didn't feel ready to die. She prayed for one more chance. *Please God, everything I did, I did it for you.* She looked over her shoulder toward Sixth Street, but nobody was there.

The cop kept walking toward her. He walked past his partner's body splayed out on the ground. She braced herself. He looked crazy. His mouth was open. He looked like he was going to cry. He held his gun loosely in his right hand.

"Please don't tell on me," he said. He walked right up to her and raised the gun up and pointed it at her head and said, "I didn't fucking do it."

All of the men that Emily had ever known passed through her mind; good men and bad men; teachers, boyfriends, and bullies.

"No," she said, her mind becoming calm and focused. Something clicked. She felt composure settle into her. "Listen to me," she said, staring him in his eyes. "I'm your witness. I saw it. You saved him. You tried to save that guy, your friend. You did right. You had to. You get it? I saw it."

Elias lowered the gun. "I don't know what to do," he said. "Jesus Christ. I'm fucked." His face was squeezed in like he smelled death. He kept up a low moaning sound.

Emily pulled on the cuff. It wouldn't budge. People had started to appear at the mouth of the alley, but they were still far away.

Elias bent over in front of her. "Oh fuck. I'm so fucked. I'm so fucked." He looked up at her and said, "I don't know what to do."

Emily breathed deeply. "Listen to me," she said. He looked at her. "Did you radio it in?"

He stopped moaning. "Fuck," he said. He sounded like a dope fiend. "My radio's in the car," he said.

"Do you have a phone?" she asked, calmly. She was in complete control now.

He patted his pockets, pulled out a cell phone, and looked at her.

"Call nine-one-one," she said. The sound of sirens was already growing in the background.

She looked at him and said, "I didn't rob that bank. You hear me? This is the deal: I didn't rob that bank. I was smoking weed right here. That man in the van tried to grab me. You and your partner saved me, right?"

Elias stopped crying. He looked at her, trying to understand.

"You saved me, right?" She looked straight at him and sounded out the words: "You saved me and I didn't rob no bank."

Elias's face relaxed; he seemed to understand. He tucked the gun behind his back and unlocked her handcuffs.

9

Emily, for the past hour, had been sitting alone in a ten-foot-by-ten-foot interview room in the homicide unit at 850 Bryant Street. The room was lit by a large fluorescent tube on the ceiling, which gave off stuttering, bright light. She could hear the low rumblings of male voices. Every now and then she heard the sound of yelling coming in through the walls. The room smelled vaguely of shit.

She had never been in an interview room before; all of her prior arrests were the type that didn't warrant formal interviews. The carpet was stained. The walls were grimy, like someone with dirty hands had been touching them. There was a table that seemed too big for the space. Electrical piping circled the room at head level. The words *fuck you* had been scrawled onto the wall to her right. The only window was a five-inch square in the door, which looked out toward a wall in the hallway.

Emily was trying to breathe deep and calm down. The fact that she had to rely on the cop was no good. He was crazy. Anybody could see that. He looked like he was on PCP.

The door opened. A woman and a man squeezed into the room. The woman wore a black, slightly wrinkled pantsuit with a pearl-colored shirt; she had long brown hair with gray in it and a deep crease in the skin between her eyes. The man was tall and bald, with a shaved head. He looked like he weighed three hundred pounds, but his suit still hung loose on his body.

The woman took the seat opposite Emily. The man said something about needing a chair and stepped back out of the room.

The lady looked at Emily's face, like she was trying to size her up. "I'm sorry we kept you waiting so long," she said.

Emily nodded.

"Can we get you a drink, or something to eat?"

"I am kind of thirsty," said Emily. *What do they know?* Emily read the woman's face for clues. *Do they know about the bank?* Emily remembered the crazy cop saying they were the only ones who knew about the bank. *I was wearing a wid and glasses,* she told herself. *I am one woman out of half a million women in San Francisco. Relax.*

The door opened, and the bald cop stepped back in carrying a plastic chair.

"Dave, can you get Ms. Rosario a . . ." She looked at Emily.

"A Coke."

"Get her a Coke."

He set the chair down and left. The woman cop leaned forward on her elbows and looked into Emily's eyes.

"Officer Sam Trammell was pronounced dead."

"I know," said Emily.

"He was a good cop. A good man."

"He seemed like it." The cop squinted. *Too much,* thought Emily. "In the short time he was helping me." *Slow down,* thought Emily.

The cop breathed in heavily and looked through some papers on the table in front of her. Emily's eyes went to the papers, pages and pages of photocopied handwritten notes. Emily couldn't make out the words. The bald cop stepped back into the room and handed Emily the Coke, which she opened shyly, as if the noise might disturb someone. The bald cop sat down next to the woman. He had to squeeze in to fit. The temperature in the room seemed to rise.

"I'm Inspector Cooley," said the lady, "and this is Inspector Lake." She nodded toward the bald cop. "Again, sorry for the wait. You understand that you're not being held here, right?"

Emily nodded, but she knew it wasn't true.

"You're free to go at any time. If you want, you can get up right now and just walk out that door." The lady cop's thumb pointed to the door behind her.

"Yeah, no, it's all good," said Emily.

"Good," said the bald cop.

The lady cop spoke. "So, Emily, I'm just going to turn on this tape player so we can tape this, and we'll get you out of here as fast as possible. I know this is really stressful." She pressed the record button on a black tape recorder that sat on the table. Emily figured the tape recorder was probably for show; there was probably a hidden camera in the corner of the ceiling, and the room would be wired for sound.

"Today's date is August second, 2010," the woman said. "The time is twenty-two-thirty. I'm Inspector Cooley, I'm here with—"

"Inspector Lake, star number 1149."

"We're in the Homicide Division, speaking with, Emily— Emily, go ahead and say your full name."

"Emily Rosario."

"What's your date of birth?"

"January eleventh, 1983."

"Now Emily, I've told you that you are not under arrest, right?"

"Yes."

"I've told you, you can walk out this door any time you want. Right?"

"Yes, ma'am."

"Okay. Now, Emily, because this incident involved the death of an officer, I have to read you your rights."

"Okay."

"You have the right to remain silent," said the female cop. "Anything you say may be used against you in a court of law. You have the right to consult an attorney. You have the right to have an attorney here with you. If you cannot afford an attorney, one will be appointed to you. Do you understand these rights?"

Emily nodded.

"I need you to say you understand them."

"I understand them," said Emily.

"Good. Okay, Emily, you witnessed an incident tonight on Minna alley."

"That's right."

"Why don't you just set the scene for us, where you were coming from, you know, that stuff."

"Okay, I had been . . ." Emily's mind tracked across her story. She hadn't considered how to answer these preliminary questions. *Where had I been?* She had been hiding in a motel because she'd robbed a bank and some Russians wanted to kill her. *Stick to the truth.* "I had been—I stay at the Auburn Hotel, you know, right there where this thing happened, but I had been gone for like a week, or something, so I had just come back." It was a long speech.

"Where had you been?" asked the bald one.

"I was staying in the Marina." *No reason not to be,* she thought.

"Okay," said the lady. "So you're coming back home, and what happens?"

Emily's eyes went from one cop's face to the other. She had to make them think they were smart; make them feel they were in control. Her eyes went to the tape machine on the table between them. *Show them fear,* she thought. *Throw out a little fear and see what they throw back.* "Can you turn the tape off for one second?" asked Emily. She put a pained look on her face.

Inspector Cooley pressed stop on the tape.

"I got a question," said Emily.

"Go ahead."

"What if what I was doing was," she paused and then continued, "you know, am I gonna get in trouble?"

Cooley's eyes smiled a little. "Emily, whatever you were doing, we're not interested in that. We don't care. We're not looking to get you in trouble."

"A cop got killed," said the bald one. "We want to know what happened."

So far, they had not shown any signs of knowing about the bank robbery. They were not coming at her hard at all. It seemed, Emily thought, looking down at the can of Coke on the table, that they genuinely wanted her to help them.

The lady cop raised her eyebrows at Emily like a question, and Emily nodded. The cop pressed the record button.

"We're back on tape," said the woman.

"Go on," said the man.

"So, I came back, and then all that stuff happened." *Play dumb. Keep it simple.* Emily breathed in and out, calming herself.

"What happened?"

"The guy, the man who grabbed me, shot the one cop, and then the other cop shot him, and that's it. That's all I know."

"Did you know the man who grabbed you?" asked the woman.

"No. Nope."

"Had you ever seen him before?"

"Not before tonight." Emily locked eyes with the female cop and felt her blood pressure rise, but to a controllable level. The cop was good, she didn't give any signs; her face didn't betray what she knew, one way or the other.

"Tell us about him trying to grab you. You know, where did he do it, what did he say?" said the female cop in a soothing way.

"He grabbed me right in that alley, right where it all went down."

The female cop's face looked concerned. Emily watched as the area in the middle of her eyebrows tensed; she saw her lips get tight. She didn't look at the bald one; she just focused on the woman. And the woman cop's face showed a slight sign of disbelief.

"Where did you first run into the man who grabbed you?" she asked again.

"In the alley."

"The problem is," said the bald one, "we know Officer Trammell and Officer Elias walked you down Sixth Street to Minna alley. We've talked to witnesses and we've seen some video, so we know that part. We're just having a hard time seeing what you're telling us."

"That's it," said Emily, "that's right, the two cops, sorry, the two officers had gotten me on Sixth Street and walked me down to Minna and over that way toward the man that had tried to grab me." The words felt jumbled. She was having a hard time finding a rhythm. *I need to quit using drugs*, she thought.

"When did the man try to grab at you?" asked the lady.

Emily understood. The timing was off. "He grabbed me before those cops had seen me." She put a little bit of annoyance into her answer to try to keep the conversation moving.

"Okay, so the cops had seen you, and they walked you *back* to where this man had tried to grab you?" asked the female cop.

Emily felt like the lady was telling her this was the right thing to say. "That's right," said Emily.

"So, how long before you ran into the cops had the man been grabbing on you?" asked the bald cop.

"Just then, just before all this."

"Now when you say 'grab,' what do you mean?"

"I mean, I was walking to my house and that punk, sorry, that man tried to grab me and pull me into his van."

"Where'd he grab you?"

"'Cause he's a pervert."

"*Where'd* he grab you?"

"He grabbed my arm." Emily raised her left arm. One half of the Russian's handcuffs—the half that remained after she shot herself free when she woke up in the park—was dangling from her wrist. She dropped her hand.

"Is that a handcuff on your wrist?" asked the bald cop.

"Yeah," said Emily.

"Why?" he asked.

"It's one of those fashion things," said Emily, "like a hip-hop thing. They got them now."

The female cop nodded her head, but her eyes looked skeptical.

"Were you ever handcuffed to a window?" asked the female.

"No, I don't think so. But my memory is all messed up over what happened."

"There's a witness who stated that you were cuffed to a wall."

"What'd the cop say?" asked Emily.

"Were you ever cuffed to a wall?" asked the female.

"Not that I could remember, unless the officer said I was. He's probably better trained at all that memorizing than me." Emily wanted to dig her heels in. She figured that maybe by arguing about a small point she could avoid any bigger questions.

The two cops stayed silent. Emily could hear a vague electrical droning all around her. She looked down at the tape player and watched the wheels turn. The flesh on her stomach hurt where the cop had pinched her. The bald cop kept staring while the female leafed through the loose papers in front of her. Emily, in an effort to appear calm, yawned.

"So, the man tried to grab you?"

"Yes."

"In the alley?"

"That's right."

"And you ran to the two officers?"

"Uh huh. I mean, I ran in their direction, but they saw me and they grabbed me. And then I told them what happened and they took me back that way. And then it was just like bang, bang, bang and that's it."

"I see," said the bald cop.

"When did you cut your hair?" asked the female cop.

"From what?" asked Emily.

"Your old mug shot, and your DMV picture, you always had longer hair."

"For a change. And to make my boyfriend mad."

"Who's your boyfriend?"

"His name's Pierre. Well, his name's Anthony Baptiste, but they call him Pierre."

"And where's he?"

"That's my question, too," said Emily.

The female cop smiled. "So, the man grabbed you, you ran to the cops, they walked you back to Minna alley. What was the man doing when you got there with the cops?"

"He was just sitting in that van with the engine on, right in the middle of the street, just hella lurking."

"And what did the two officers do?"

"They walked to the van to get him like that, or talk to him, you know, that kind of thing, but the dude just opened the door and straight walked right at them and raised up."

"He fired his weapon?"

"Straight ringing bells, shot the young cop and then *boom*, the other cop shot him. It all went down in a second. Just like that: *bang, bang*. But he saved me, the officer did. I wish I could thank him, though." The words were coming free and easy now. She took a sip from the Coke can.

"And you were handcuffed at this time?"

"Not that I recall, but if that cop says I was then he probably knows better than I do." The officers stayed silent. "He's the hero, not me," said Emily. Emily and the female cop locked eyes. Emily didn't look away.

"Did the man say anything as he raised his weapon?"

"The Russian?" asked Emily. As it came out of her mouth she wanted to grab the words and pull them back in, but she couldn't; they had escaped and the little black tape recorder on the table continued to turn its wheels. There was nothing she could do. She tried to compose her face. She could feel tiny sweat clouds forming on her brow.

"The man," said the bald cop.

"Yep," said Emily.

"Why'd you say Russian?"

"'Cause when he had grabbed me he was like saying, *Get in the car,* but he said it like hella Russian sounding, I don't know. French, or something. Why? He ain't Russian?"

"He was a Russian citizen," said the female.

"I don't know," said Emily, shaking her head. "He's French?"

"Did he say anything to you?" asked the bald cop.

"Because his accent," said Emily. "Did he say anything? He was just like, *Get in the car, bitch.*"

"Okay," said the female, "slow down. Let me get this straight. You're coming home and the man tried to grab you, correct?"

"Yes."

"Where were you when he tried to grab you?"

"I was somewhere around there, just on my way back home."

"Was he driving in his van?"

"Yes."

"Did he stop and get out?"

"Uh huh."

"And he tried to pull you toward the van?"

"He grabbed my arm and yanked on me."

"And you managed to escape, and you ran up Sixth Street, and those officers happened to see you running, distressed, and they grabbed you?"

"That's it."

"And what did they say to you, when they grabbed you?"

"'Can we help you.'"

The space above the female cop's eyes quivered.

"No, that's not what they said, but that's what they *meant*," said Emily. The female cop nodded her head slightly. "Their actions said, can I help you."

"But they had stopped *you* as a suspect," said the bald one.

"That's right, or they stopped me 'cause I was running and that don't look right on Sixth Street."

"And you told them what had happened, with this Russian man trying to grab you."

"That's it."

"Now, you walked back with the two officers, they took you to Minna alley, they asked you to wait, because the van was there—I don't want to put words in your mouth."

"You're saying it how it was," said Emily.

"They approached the van and the dude jumped out and started shooting."

"That's it."

10

The police came. Then more. Then the ambulances. The first cops were soon joined by inspectors, crime scene investigators, sergeants, two lieutenants, and a captain. The alley became filled with men. There must have been nearly forty officers.

Someone had produced a metal folding chair and placed it right near the spot where Emily had been standing and Elias now sat on it. Trammell was dead. Elias watched everything. He was in shock. Trammell was dead and it was Elias's own fault.

Nothing made sense. Breathing was difficult. He wanted to cry. His body felt wrung out. All the drinking, all the lack of sleep, was catching up to him. The buildings, the cement, San Francisco itself, the trash, everything was making him sick. He kept taking big, exaggerated breaths, hoping something would give, but it wouldn't. He was stuck with himself.

Two of his partners from the Gang Task Force stood in front of him as a sort of barricade. They both held a hand on his shoulder, and they took turns looking at him and shaking their heads. They couldn't believe it.

His fear of being caught was making his face ache. The muscles in his shoulders felt hardened to metal. If he could just have the last week back; he would trade everything for the last week. His head ached. The foreclosure of his house occurred to him like a sick joke. Take it, he didn't care. Take his job. Take everything. *Just don't let me get caught.*

He could still feel the way his gun had recoiled when he'd shot it. It was the first time he'd ever fired his gun in action. His head and arm echoed with the buck of the gun. His ear throbbed.

He could still feel, in the memory of his finger and thumb, the place where he had pinched the girl. What would she say? How in the world did he end up in a partnership with her? Who the fuck was she?

Trammell's body had been covered with a blanket. The bullet had entered his face, above his cheek. Elias felt a desire to yell; he felt obligated to yell. He wanted to yell that Trammell shouldn't be left out on the ground like that. He figured he should be protesting somehow, exhibiting some kind of outrage, but he also felt a strange, depressed kind of stage fright. He had lost his voice. He was in shock.

He thought about confessing. He wanted to do it right away. Get it over with. Lay it all out. The pain in his chest was suffocating. He'd take the blame for everything, even for Rada Harkov. But as more officers arrived, something changed. The cops had a look in their eyes. They ran around busy and intent, but each one looked at him differently. They looked at him with something like respect. He was a man who shot a cop killer from fifteen yards away. A perfect shot.

PATRICK HOFFMAN
The cops had already taken Emily Rosario away. *You saved me, and I didn't rob no bank. You saved me.*

Inspector Ortiz was the officer in charge of the investigation and the fourth cop to ask Elias what happened. He was small and old and looked like a television cop. He ushered Elias away from his two partners and walked him farther into the alley. His manner was calm. He was a good listener.

Duda Rue. Elias explained that they had been looking for a bad guy named Duda Rue. They got a tip that he was staying at the Henry Hotel. That's where they were headed when they saw the girl running. She ran right at them. They stopped her to see what was up.

"Why was your car parked in the number-two lane?" asked Ortiz.

"'Cause we saw her running," said Elias. Committing to the lie brought a measure of calmness.

Elias could see the problems with the story even as he told it. He left out seeing the van drive by. How many witnesses were being questioned right then? How could the man in the van have grabbed her if he was driving by? Elias could feel the weight of the girl's gun in his jacket pocket; he could feel the stack of hundred-dollar bills.

"We saw the witness, the Rosario woman running up Sixth Street; we jumped out and secured information on the suspect."

Ortiz kept listening. Elias told him that they walked Emily up Sixth Street. They approached the van. The guy jumped out, and they engaged him. Ortiz nodded his head while he listened. *We engaged him.*

"The man shot Sam, and I shot him."

216

They took Elias to the Hall of Justice. He rode in the front seat, a sergeant from Southern Station drove; the sergeant didn't talk, he just kept shaking his head and wincing. Elias consciously willed himself to appear more sad. He was feeling a lot of things, but not sadness. He closed his eyes. Trammell had been shot in the cheek, below the eye, as though he had turned his head away from the gun. There was a black hole stamped in his cheek. *Rada Harkov, Sam Trammell.*

When they arrived at the Hall of Justice the sergeant pulled the car into the sally port. Lieutenant Fleming was waiting by the door with three other officers, and the group converged on the car as it stopped. The lieutenant, a man Elias had never spoken two words with, opened the car door, pulled Elias out by the arm, wrapped him in a bear hug, and squeezed him for a few seconds. "I'm so sorry," he said, and then he let go. Elias stepped back and they regarded each other. The lieutenant's eyes were filled with tears.

The group moved toward the building. "This is what's going to happen," said the lieutenant. "I already talked to Ortiz; he filled me in on everything. Delgado is waiting upstairs. He needs to talk to you before Ann gets here." Delgado was the police union rep, and Ann was the defense attorney hired by the union to represent any officer who found himself in a potentially criminal situation.

All six of the men crammed into the elevator. Elias's hand went to the outside of his pockets. He could feel the bulge of the stack of money he had taken from the girl.

Lieutenant Fleming leaned his head toward Elias and said, "Ortiz told me that you and Sam walked with the female to the alley and the suspect fired on you."

"That's right," said Elias.

The lieutenant leaned in even closer and half whispered, "Look, you've been through the wringer, and you're going to come out in one piece—don't worry about anything—but just to set me straight, tell me why you were even on Sixth Street?"

"We were 10-71 at the Henry Hotel."

"That's what Ortiz said. And the girl?"

The elevator doors opened and they walked toward the homicide department.

"We saw her running. Trammell went after her—I don't even know why—on a hunch, I guess. She told him a man had tried to grab her in the alley, and we walked her back over there in an attempt to locate the suspect." Elias felt a wave of fear. *Was this story crazy?*

"The woman was in distress?" said the lieutenant.

"That's right."

"I just wanted to hear it in your own words."

"Distress," said Elias.

The lieutenant clapped him on the back and handed him off to John Delgado, who was waiting at the door of the homicide unit.

Delgado was wearing jeans and a sweater. He looked like an unemployed father. He was rumpled and in need of a haircut. He walked Elias away from the other officers and down the hall. "Jesus," he said. "Un-fucking-believable. I'm sorry. Don't worry, we're just waiting on Ann Richter to get here. You're going to have to sit down with some inspectors from Homicide and tell the story one more time. That's it. We'll run through it together with Ann, make sure everything's good, but from what I've heard you're fine. You've got nothing to worry about. Shit, you should get a promotion."

"It's Sam who should get the promotion."

"Commendation."

"He saved me."

"Worst day of your fucking life."

Delgado leaned toward Elias and whispered, "There were a couple cameras in the alley, but none of them caught the incident. Which is to say, your memory of what happened is the correct version. Also, just so you know, there were a couple cameras on Sixth Street that got you walking the girl toward the alley. But that's it."

Elias nodded.

Ann Richter came. She talked with Elias and Delgado in the hallway. She was reassuringly unfriendly. She hadn't changed out of her work clothes, and she looked tired. Elias smelled wine, garlic, and seafood on her breath. She didn't seem concerned about him.

When they were ready, they walked back down the hallway and into the homicide unit. Elias had only been here a few times. They walked past a row of interview rooms. He saw Emily Rosario waiting in one of them. She had her head down on the table in front of her and didn't appear to notice him.

The interview was conducted in the lieutenant's office. The lieutenant waited outside the room with Delgado. Ann Richter sat behind Elias. A female inspector named Cooley and her partner, Lake, had him tell the story one more time. Ann Richter didn't speak except to identify herself for the tape.

He told the story the same way he had told it to everybody else. The words came out easily. He wasn't challenged on any points. Everything was pro forma. Emily Rosario had given him his lines, and now he used them.

As he talked, all of the wildness that he had been feeling over the last week, over the last few months, all of the instability vanished; for the first time in ages, he felt calm. Even the gun and the money didn't bother him.

The interview ended. Elias, stepping out of the lieutenant's office, felt a wave of importance. He felt at the center of things. He shook hands with Ann Richter. Her hand lingered in his for a moment.

Delgado and the lieutenant walked him down the hallway, toward the elevator. They were joined by a young, uniformed female officer.

"Carbonza's going to drive you home," said the lieutenant, nodding at the female. "I want you to call this number tomorrow." He handed Elias a Post-it note with a number handwritten on it. "Set up a time to talk with him. He's a good guy. You're going to need to talk about this stuff. That's an order." The lieutenant reached out and shook Elias's hand one final time.

"Yes, sir," said Elias. He stared at the Post-it.

The female officer drove, and Elias rode up front. They rode in silence until he asked her how she liked being on the force. She was so young. Elias felt like this drive could be one of those moments she remembered forever. She told him it was great.

"Busy," she added. "It gets hectic—like today, they got your thing, they got a shooting in Double Rock, and they got that dead lady in McLaren Park."

They had found Rada Harkov's body and in that moment, with the freeway coming at him, he was sure they would find him, too.

11

Emily rode the elevator down to the ground floor of the Hall of Justice. The female inspector had shaken her awake in the interview room and told her she could leave. When Emily asked if it was all right to go home, the inspector, her face showing a mix of cynicism and confusion, had said, "Why wouldn't it be?"

The sheriff's deputies at the front entrance of the building stared dumbly at Emily as she left. She walked down the front stairs to the sidewalk on Bryant Street. There was nobody around; the street was deserted and the temperature had dropped. Emily finally understood once and for all that it was time to leave San Francisco. *Fuck Pierre, fuck everyone,* it was time to go.

She cut through the McDonald's parking lot. It was empty but for two dark cars occupied by men who chewed and stared and didn't look away. The wind pushed trash over the ground. A car alarm sounded in the distance. She passed a homeless man who was staring in the direction from which she had come; his face—with his lips pursed round, the inside of his eyebrows tucked in, and his head tilted to the side—all suggested he was seeing something behind her. She turned and looked: there was nothing.

She crossed Sixth Street, picked up her pace, and headed under the freeway overpass. The noise of the cars driving above sounded like landing airplanes. It was dark down there; the columns, painted mint green and stained dirty, were large enough to hide a gang of men. The sidewalks were bordered by fences topped with barbed wire, and the sidewalks themselves were stained brown. Emily didn't know what time it was, but traffic on Sixth Street was light. She pulled her jacket in to try to warm up.

Emily's thoughts bounced from Pierre, to her room, to her neighbor Isaac, to another neighbor named Doris, who had told her a story about a time when she had been staying at the homeless shelter at Fifth and Bryant and two of the night workers had grabbed her and tried to pull her into a utility closet. Doris, illustrating the story with full reenactments in the hallway outside Emily's room, had told Emily that she managed to fight them off by using her thumbnails as knives and aiming at their eyes. Emily pictured Doris laughing: her bottom front teeth were missing; she had wrinkle lines around her mouth; she held her thumbs out like hooks and danced around like a boxer. Doris later got arrested for selling pills and had to move to a halfway house in Manteca. She had called Emily from jail and told her to hold all her stuff for her. Emily went to her room to get her things but found that someone else had already been there and taken all the good stuff.

Emily rubbed her own thumbnails and was sad to feel them bitten down to nubs.

A man on a bicycle rode past and called out, "I got pills." Much later, Emily tried to reconstruct in her head the scene that followed so that she could somehow understand where the different players had come from. She was still under the freeway. She remembered a black Monte Carlo driving past on the opposite side of the street (headed away from downtown), the sound of heavy bass droning from the trunk. The Monte Carlo was up on twenty-twos and if Emily turned and watched it as it went, it wasn't based on caution, but more because she wanted that specific car for herself. In her memory that was the only car that had passed.

After following the car with her eyes she looked over her shoulder and noticed a man walking behind her. He was thirty feet away when she first saw him. Later, she tried to remember if she had seen him cross to her side of the street, or if he had been waiting on Bryant. Had the homeless man she walked past been staring at this guy? Who had the man on the bike been offering pills to? And if Emily had stopped the man on the bike, what would have happened?

It seemed to have become even darker where she was. The man on the bike had turned onto Harrison and was gone. The Monte Carlo was gone. Emily's instinct to run set in. The thought *I will quit drugs* played through her mind. *I will leave the city.* Even under these circumstances Emily recognized that her desire to quit drugs always seemed to kick in when she found herself in some kind of dire situation. She thought of her friend Jules Gunn and pictured them together somewhere warm.

The man behind her was silhouetted by lights, so Emily couldn't see his face, but the way he was moving, the determination of his walk, made the hollowed-out feeling of fear in her gut grow in mass. She thought of buses, first wishing there was one on Sixth Street, and then thinking about Greyhounds and wishing she was on one. She tried to speed up, but she felt like she was in a dream, like her feet would not move as fast as she needed them to. She looked around for help but there was nobody. The nearest open business, lit up like a kind of sanctuary, was the gas station at the corner of Sixth and Harrison. Nobody was outside pumping gas. It was only about six hundred feet away but it felt like miles.

The man was getting closer. Cars passed indifferently and for a moment Emily pictured exactly what she looked like to the passing drivers: poor and loud. Only men were out, only lurking men were out at this time; it felt to Emily like she was the last woman on earth. Fear tangled her limbs. The smell of urine was everywhere. Flies swarmed around a spot on the sidewalk and up at her face; the ground beneath her shook from the cars driving on the freeway overhead. Images of the cop getting shot, his head snapping back, the Russian getting shot, all looped through her mind.

Emily stepped toward the street, ready to run into the middle of traffic if she needed to. The man was closer now. Emily turned and watched as he came. She squared up to him, not wanting to turn her back. He was fifteen feet from her. Her hand instinctively went to where the gun had been, but she remembered the cops had taken it. She raised her fists up to her stomach and turned and stepped off the curb to let the man pass, but instead he came right at her.

Confusion set in. Pierre? *Pierre. Pierre. Pierre.* It wasn't happiness that she felt upon seeing him, with his low hairline and bugged eyes, his skinny arms out all arrogant; instead she felt an immediate surge of anger. She could tell he was mad. She could tell he thought that he was saving her. He closed in on her.

"What the fuck you do?" he yelled. His face looked angry and ugly. Spit came out of his mouth.

Her anger instantly matched his. "That's how you're gonna do this?" she yelled back.

"What the fuck you do?" he yelled again, emphasizing the words *you* and *do*, as though that would somehow make the question more clear. He moved closer, like he was going to tackle her. "You know what you did!"

She stepped back, but he grabbed on to both her arms and crushed down on them. She didn't understand what was happening. She tried to pull away, but she couldn't. His hands were locked down on hers. She could feel his nails digging into the skin of her wrists. Cars drove past in both directions, but nobody stopped.

"What the fuck you get me in?" he yelled. He seemed high and drunk.

"Let me go," was all she could answer.

A car slowed down and stopped near the curb. Emily leaned toward it and again tried to squirm out of Pierre's grip. He swung her toward the car. The driver's door opened and a man stepped out.

"Help me," said Emily.

The man walked around the front of the car. Emily recognized him: it was the man from the alley. The private investigator, Nichols.

"Help me!" Emily said to him. Her arms were held down. She couldn't wave for help. "No, no, no," said Emily. She was terrified. Pierre was pulling her toward the car. The man, Nichols, walked right at them.

"Get in the car," said Nichols.

Pierre opened the back door and began to push Emily in. She fought against him, but he was too strong. He forced her head into the car and then Emily saw Sophia, sitting in the back, her face looking so scared that Emily thought maybe she had been kidnapped, too. There was a gun in Sophia's hand, though, and Emily knew it was bad. The gun shook in the woman's hand. Emily was forced all the way in. The door shoved shut behind her.

Pierre grabbed at the front passenger door, trying to open it, but it was locked. The whole car shook. Pierre started banging at Emily's window, leaving little smears on the glass. Nothing made sense. Emily watched as the bald man, Nichols, stepped behind Pierre and held something to his neck; Pierre's body jolted up straight and then slumped down to the ground. The man stepped over Pierre, picked up his legs, and moved him out of the road. He then went back up to Pierre's head and held the Taser to his neck. Pierre's body twitched and shook. The man then walked to the driver's side and jumped into the car.

"Fuck you," said Emily. "Damn, y'all, fuck!"

Sophia held the gun at her. Emily looked at Sophia. Her bangs were straight, she was wearing the same wine-colored lipstick as before, she had her glasses on, but underneath it all Emily sensed panic.

"Calm down," said Nichols. He breathed heavily and leaned over in his seat toward the passenger window to try to look at Pierre. He turned and looked at Sophia and Emily, fastened his seat belt, and wheeled the car back into traffic.

"I didn't ask for this," said Emily. She looked out the back window at Pierre lying on the sidewalk as they drove away. "I don't even want your stupid fucking money."

"Of course you don't," said Sophia. "It's not yours. How could you want what's not yours?"

"I don't even need my little percentile."

"You don't get a percent!" said Sophia. "You understand? You stupid fucking American junky." The car bumped as they went. Sophia reached out and grabbed Emily's chin, and held it gently. "I'm sorry, I'm sorry to yell," she said. She breathed deeply like she was composing herself and said, "We need the money. No more games."

"It's in my room," said Emily. She was done with Pierre. She was done with San Francisco.

Nichols looked at her in the rearview mirror as he drove. "Don't worry about Pierre. I just shocked him."

Fuck him, thought Emily.

"It's not his fault," said Nichols. "We made him do it. He didn't have a choice."

"I don't give a fuck," said Emily.

They stopped at a red light. "Let me tell you something," said Sophia. "When I was a young girl in my country, I got caught stealing packages of cigarettes from one of our bosses. He was a very mean man, big and ugly, but he worked with my father. When he caught me he told me, 'Stealing is an art, but there are certain things you never steal, and certain people you never steal from'—he didn't hurt me but he said—'don't steal what you can't sell, and don't steal from anyone who would enjoy cutting your hand off.' He was a stupid man, and I continued to steal from him, but I think his lesson may be an appropriate one for you to consider." The light turned green.

They drove down Sixth Street past Minna alley. There were still police officers and yellow tape everywhere; it was madness to come back here. Nichols drove around the block and made a right onto Mission Street. A man was praying like a Muslim on the sidewalk. They continued to Fifth Street, made a right, and parked the car.

"We can't go in there now," said Emily.

Sophia pushed the gun into Emily's side. "At some point," Sophia said, "you are going to come to realize that you are not telling us what to do." She stopped talking and looked around like she was checking for witnesses.

The phrase *I'm the boss* popped into Emily's mind. It wasn't that she was feeling it, invoking it, or anything—it just came. It was followed by: *I tell bitches what to do.*

"The cops are everywhere," said Emily. She was conscious that they were going to make her go, but she wanted to create the illusion that they were in control.

"Emily," said Nichols, "we're going to walk in right past those cops. Okay? If you make a move, if you say anything, I won't kill you, it's not like that now." He shook his head like someone uninterested in buying shoes from a homeless man. "I'll just calmly walk up and tell them that you're the woman who robbed the bank. And this is the point that will really piss them off: I'll tell them that you're the reason their little buddy got killed. I wasn't even here," he said, looking back at her in the mirror. "I'll get a reward."

Emily sat with her head down.

"Now are you ready to fix it?" he asked.

"Yes," she said.

"You gave a statement at the station," Nichols said. "Tell me the name of the detectives you talked to."

Emily pulled out a business card from her pocket and gave it to him. He read it and put it in his breast pocket.

"Let's go," said Nichols.

They walked down Minna alley. At the police tape, a walrus-looking cop was staring like he was ready to arrest them. Nichols, composed and authoritative, explained that Emily was a witness to the shooting, and that Inspector Cooley had asked them to take her home. He pointed toward the Auburn, which was between them and the actual crime scene. The cop called over a younger cop and asked him to walk the three of them to the door of the hotel. "Don't linger," said the walrus cop.

The young cop walked in front. He seemed bored. Emily wondered what would happen if she ran. Nothing good. There weren't that many cops out anymore. There was a man snapping pictures of something on the ground, and just past him a man took measurements. The other cops just stood at different spots, or walked from here to there.

The young cop held his hand to the front door of the Auburn like a waiter seating them at a table. Emily, with Nichols and Sophia following right behind, walked up the stairs to the door, realized she didn't have her keys, and was buzzed in.

The manager looked happy to see her. "Where you been?" he asked. His eyes went from Emily to the other two and back again. "Everyone's been looking for you."

"Tell them I'm gone," she said. She signed her two guests in and got a key for her room from the manager. The whole process seemed absurd. Sophia had become shy. Nichols was clenched.

They walked up to the third floor. Emily's heart was beating so hard it seemed to interfere with her breathing. She had to pull herself along on the rails to keep going. *I will stop doing bad things. I will clean up.*

The air smelled stale. Emily had a rising hatred for this place, for her life, for everybody and everything. Nobody else was in the hallway. The place seemed unusually quiet. She realized she had spent her entire life being told what to do.

At her door, Emily put the key into the lock and felt it slide into place. She looked back at Sophia and Nichols. They looked pathetic, scared themselves. Emily decided right then that they weren't monsters. They could be ripped off just like anyone else.

She breathed deep and opened the door and flicked the light switch and the room lit up. Pierre's neat little room. She could smell him in there and she realized she didn't like the smell. It had never been her home.

She stepped in and the other two crowded in behind her and closed the door. Emily's mouth was dry. She could see the red and blue light from the police cars out her window. Water ran through the pipes over her head. She pointed toward the bed.

"I checked there," said Nichols.

PATRICK HOFFMAN

"Check again."

He moved to the bed and pulled the mattress off the bed frame. The black bag from Walgreens sat there like a prize.

Nichols exhaled. He looked at Emily, smiled, stepped toward the bag, and pulled it up off the ground. He felt the weight in his hand and then he walked to the desk and set it down. "Watch her," he said to Sophia.

He unzipped it and looked. The bills, stacked and green, were a beautiful sight. He reached his hand in and pushed the money around. Emily, knowing that his examination of the bag had to be stopped, took a step toward him. The balance of the room shifted. Nichols turned toward her.

"Give me it," said Sophia. She had the gun out again. She looked unhinged.

"We'll split it," said Emily, purposefully hitting a higher note to signify desperation. She finally felt natural. She could see where she wanted things to go, and she knew exactly how to get them there. She needed just one more chance.

Nichols zipped the bag closed and turned toward the door.

Sophia raised the gun up and said, "No, no, no, give it to me."

Nichols didn't do anything. He stood there and waited. Sophia pulled the trigger and the hammer clicked down, but nothing happened. She pulled it again and again and the thing kept clicking.

"You fucking cunt, you think I'd give you a loaded gun?" said Nichols.

He walked toward the door. Sophia sprung on him and started scratching at his face. She was making a high-pitched, animal noise. They thrashed toward the wall. Nichols managed to get a hold of her hair, and forced her head down to the ground and held it against the floor. He was telling her to shut up. He put his weight on her head until she stopped fighting and then he got up and looked around wildly like he'd realized Emily might jump on him. He grabbed the black bag and stepped out of the room, closing the door shut as he went.

Emily looked at Sophia. She had pushed herself up to a seated position. Her glasses were off, her hair was crazy, blood was smeared around her nose and mouth. She was breathing heavy, her back against the wall, and Emily felt a wave of compassion. It wasn't Sophia's fault; it wasn't anybody's fault. Things sometimes just got out of control.

JULES GUNN'S EPILOGUE

Emily called me that night, told me to pack my bags and pick her up, we going on a trip, she said. She said, Jules, pick me up right now, come to the Kingsley Hotel, right near the Auburn, right on Howard Street, pick me up. Her voice was hella crazy and I knew even before she told me that this was gonna be about some real money shit. She said, pick me up right now. And I did.

I jumped in the Escalade and within a half hour I had her in the car and we were on the Bay Bridge and she was already telling me how she had robbed that bank. She told me the whole damn thing before we were even an hour outside of the city. Told me all about the Russians and how they were drugging her and how they made her do it. Told me how she told those Russian motherfuckers, hell no. Told me she took the money for her damn self. She said, hell no, I'm a grimy bitch, and you don't push a grimy bitch. She told me about Pierre. She told me about the Russian lady. She told me about the bald white dude in the car. She told me about the cops, and how one of them got killed right in front of her and how she had to tell the other one what to do. Told me a Russian boy got shot, too. Told me about the showdown in the room. Told me she got them with the old switcheroo. Told me she left that Russian lady in the room, went to her neighbor's, grabbed her money bag from his ceiling, went up on the roof, and crossed over to the other hotel and called me. She talked hella fast. She told me it all.

I asked her why she didn't tell me any of it when she had me bring out the dollar bills to the hotel; I told her we could have left right then. All she could say was to shake her head and say she didn't know, said she still wasn't right in her head.

We drove straight to Las Vegas. I took us to the Hard Rock. Checked in at a nice hotel. Had a room with a view. I wasn't tripping on it though, but she was. She was nervous as hell. We got drunk down at the bar and ended up sleeping in the same bed. Best friends, or not, she knew it was on. She knew what she was doing. I always knew she wanted it.

We stayed in Las Vegas for three nights. Went to the Bellagio, ate all-you-could-eat crab legs. We had money, too. We went shopping. Took my ass to the Marni store. She was spending hella money on me. Bought me dresses. But she didn't want none of that. She just wanted some jeans, some Nikes, and some clean white T-shirts. It always makes me laugh how a girl could go dyke and decide she was on some man clothes shit straight out the gate.

We bought me makeup. Got me a bag at the Marc Jacobs store. Got the whip detailed. Put in a new stereo, put in some new speakers. We ate all the good food. Didn't even barely gamble; just played the slots a little. Emily was walking around holding my hand acting like she had always been gay. She was on some Sinatra shit, too, talking about, It had to be you.

After that we headed for Miami. Drove all the way to Dallas in one day. We'd stop at the rest stops and smoke cigarettes 'cause I try not to smoke in the Escalade. We stayed downtown at another hotel, ate the food, looked in at some shops.

From Dallas we drove to New Orleans. Emily had never even left California before, so she was really tripping off New Orleans. I showed her it. I know it. I been there. We stayed there for another three days. I know a girl named Lady that dances at Big Daddy's and she took us all over the town. We were drunk the whole time. We'd get so drunk that we'd end up fighting, but by the morning we'd forget what we'd been fighting about in the first place.

We got tattoos, too. The shop had a poster of Russian prison tattoos; Emily saw it and lit up. She picked out a tom cat with a top hat, a bow tie, paws and claws, and underneath the words, Help Your Self; it was supposed to mean she was a thief. She got it on her left forearm. She seemed real proud of that one. I got an old-looking kind of sailing ship, a vessel, it was supposed to mean escape. It was Russian, too, but I always liked ships, so I didn't care.

Emily liked New Orleans; said she was tempted to have us stay there. She liked all the food and the people, the partying, the music, all of it. But I convinced her to keep on coming to Miami, see my family, see where I came from.

We drove straight from New Orleans all the way to Miami. Emily was hungover and acting grumpy, but I could tell she was tripping off the clouds and the warm air. We'd listen to music, roll the windows down, play us some Sade, hold hands, we were acting hella stupid.

We got to Miami, got to Liberty City, that's where I'm from, got our welcoming party from my mom and all of them. Liberty

City's a rough-ass place, though. Emily said it looked like a tropical Sunnydale. All the people thought she was Chinese. Emily was the only nonblack person in the city. She got drunk at the party and tried to show them she could rap, talking about:

I'm a boss bitch. I'm a bad bitch. I took money from a bank then I switch shit. I'm a rich bitch, with a bad bitch. I got Jules on my wrist 'cause I took shit. I talk shit. I bought shit. I'm 'bout shit, 'cause I'm a boss bitch.

She made my little nieces and nephews laugh too hard at that one. She was making everyone laugh. The warm weather was turning her into a regular Katt Williams.

We rented a little apartment over near Legion Park. My uncle knew someone who knew someone and we paid cash for a fully furnished one-bedroom. Emily said it was the biggest place she had ever lived. She would strut around the living room nodding her head. The streets were green and quiet. We'd walk around, drink gin, smoke cigarettes, try to be healthy.

I was teaching Emily yoga. I learned it in prison—we had a girl named Lisa in Chowchilla, that volunteered and came and taught the inmates. I'd tell Emily: You got seventy-two thousand rivers of energy running through your body. Seventy-two thousand tunnels of light. Breathe in and breathe out. Leave all of your worries out the door. Breathe in and breathe out. You are in the place you need to be. You are where you need to be. Everything comes and everything goes. Let the light run through you. Don't think too much, just be in your body. Let yourself be here in this body, in this place, right now. Freedom. Freedom. I'd show her the downward dog, show her corpse pose, all of it. She liked it. She'd do it in the living room wearing sweat shorts and a wifebeater.

I got us healthy, too. I told her no more pills. No more coke. We'd be off an ecstasy on a special occasion like my cousin's birthday party, but that was it. No more pain pills. We'd smoke weed and drink, but no more pills like that. I'd make her drink juice with ginger in it; she'd act like she didn't like it, but I knew she did. She was looking good, too; we both were. Sunshine will do that to you.

We followed what was going on back in San Francisco, too. It looked like all hell broke loose after we left. Turned into a national news story. They had them up on CNN talking about a Russian crime war. First, there was the ugly Russian boy that got shot by the cop in front of Emily. Then that same day they found the lady bank manager dead in the park. Emily said she could barely even remember meeting that one. After that the bodies really started piling up. The news said an old man by the name of Yakov Radionovich got killed in broad daylight outside a Russian teahouse in the Richmond. They shot the man in his head and then cut off his hand with an ax. They were on some real revenge-type shit out there. Three, four more Russians got killed that week. Buildings in the Richmond got burnt down. Emily said she knew it was the lady Sophia doing it. I had my own sources who were telling me that a Russian lady did in fact take over. They didn't have no details, but the streets whisper and they were whispering loud about a Russian lady.

Don't scorn a bitch, said Emily, shaking her head like she knew all kinds of things. Don't scorn a bitch.

We watched that cop, too. He was all in the news himself. They kept writing stories about him, calling him hero cop and all that. The paper would say: Leo Elias, hero cop, loses house to foreclosure. Then the next article was saying: Police union comes together to save hero cop's house. They showed pictures of him, too. My mom's mom was Haitian and she taught me how to read people's face, and that man's face did not look happy, saved house, or not; his face looked fake as a motherfucker. Looked like he didn't want to be at any of the celebrations they were throwing him. I showed the pictures to Emily, and she'd say, Well, even if the man did pinch my stomach and talk hella shit, he didn't tell on me, so we cool.

A few months of hanging out, doing our thing and both of us started to get a little antsy. Problem is, the both of us are born hustlers. All we ever did was try to hustle to survive, hustle to get drugs, hustle to find a place to stay; as soon as we had all that taken care of we were left with a void in our lives. All the yoga, sun, and juice in the world can't fill that void.

Soon, we were making all kinds of plans. Emily said she'd take all the money she had and flip it for some drugs. Said she'd give all $800,000 to the person who could give us thirty pounds of that pure Israeli ecstasy. Nobody could say no to a deal like that—we were offering twice the going rate. We could turn the thirty pounds into about 150,000 pills. Shit, we'd turn that to a million-and-two—go back and repeat. Get our foot in the door. My cousin knew a dude in South Beach named Semion Rosenstein that could procure that much. My cousin told us the dude is Russian, which Emily obviously didn't like, but we figured the world's a big place, and they got Russians up in every corner of it.

The thing is, if you got money and a supply, you could get rich in Miami. We wouldn't even have to step out on the streets and sell it. I had all kinds of people ready to do that. I know strippers in Miami. I know hustlers in Miami. We figured once we wait for a minute, give it a year or two, we could move our operation back to San Francisco. Go west. Spread our wings and fly. This shit ain't a movie. We ain't about retiring on a beach. Everybody needs to work. Everybody gotta stay busy.

ACKNOWLEDGMENTS

I'd like to thank my agent and friend, Charlotte Sheedy, my editor, Morgan Entrekin, Patsy Wagner, and all the wonderful people at Grove Atlantic.

Ed Loftus gave me a speech that got me going. Andrew Koltuniak inspired me with his stories. Greg Jowdy helped me finish. Basho Mosko, Dante Ortiz, and Nathan Burazer talked with me every weekend. I want to thank the whole Korngold/Beinfield family, but especially Bear, Shem, and Murray, who read the manuscript and supported me with their friendship. Michelle Quint, Avi Lessing, Eric Rosenblum, David Hoffman, Brigid Hoffman, and Kent Lam also read and provided valuable feedback.

Jordan Bass, in an act of kindness I will never forget, edited an early version. Sarah Lannan, Simon Evans, Billy McEwan, Brendan Morse, E.G., Ali Nelson, Becca Nelson, Jane Rogers, and Kent Simpson always encouraged me.

I want to thank both sides of my family, but in particular, my mother, Kathy Coyne.

And, finally, I could have never written this book without the help, inspiration, and love of Reyhan Harmanci.